THE SPIDER:
RULE OF THE MONSTER MEN

THE MASTER OF MEN! SPIDER®

RULE OF THE MONSTER MEN

By Grant Stockbridge

POPULAR PUBLICATIONS • 2023

CHAPTER 1
MONSTER MAN

THE WHOLE thing actually began with the dog ambulance. It was true that Richard Wentworth had noticed an increasing number of crippled beggars on the streets, men and women with frantic, haggard faces and hideously twisted limbs. The sight of them stirred him to pity, though once he had had to drive three of them from an attack upon a pedestrian. They had scuttled off into the dark like maimed rats....

But it was the dog ambulance that played the prologue to horror.

Richard Wentworth did not at first notice the dog ambulance when it wheeled past his parked roadster. He had just seated his fiancée after an evening at the Forty-nine Club and was fumbling at the ignition switch in the darkness. By accident, he switched on the headlights and their broad blade slashed aside the blackness of the night. It cut across the dog wagon and, at his side, Nita van Sloan cried out in a shocked voice.

Wentworth's head jerked toward her and saw the startled wideness of her eyes fixed on the truck as it whipped around the far corner. "Dick," she whispered. "That dog wagon! It was full of... *of human beings!*"

Wentworth echoed blankly; "Human beings?" It was reflex rather than conscious thought that sent his roadster sweeping from the curb and set the powerful Hispano-Suiza motor humming in swift pursuit. "But why, Nita," he asked quietly, "should that have made you cry out?"

Nita shuddered and plucked her velvet cloak more closely about her bare shoulders... though the June night was very warm. "You didn't see them, Dick!" she whispered. "The back door was covered with steel wire and I looked through it expecting to see... well, to see dogs! And I couldn't see through at all. From floor to roof, there were nothing but human faces pressed tightly against the wire, hands clutching at it. A dozen of them, a score of them in that tiny space, and all fighting to breathe at that narrow door. It was exactly as if they had been captured like dogs and were being taken, like stray animals, to—*to be destroyed!*"

The Hispano's tires moaned at the turn and Wentworth sent his keen glance probing ahead, caught the glint of the ambulance whirling the next corner—caught too, the blur of white that were men's faces pressed against the wire grating. He swore under his breath, and whipped into the street in the wake of the dog wagon. A low wailing sound came to his ears, soaring with the hopeless mourning quality of an animal in pain.

"Open the gun compartment," Wentworth said steadily, his voice without expression. "I'm going to find out the meaning of this."

Nita pressed studs in the frame of the right door and a panel swung out, revealing four automatics clipped to it. Swiftly, and with expert hands, she checked their loading and placed them on the seat.

She said, hesitantly, "But, Dick, it may be the police."

2

The raiding cripples had become an army!

Richard Wentworth made no answer. His jaw had a set and determined line and his lips were thin with compression. For all her dread, Nita's full mouth softened in a smile. After these years, she should know that no fear could turn this man of hers aside from a purpose, once it was formed—and that any human being in pain or in misery could call him to battle against oppression no matter in what circumstances the cry reached him; no matter what the cost to himself....

THE GRIP of the brakes, thrusting her forward in the seat, pulled her eyes sharply forward again. The dog ambulance had stopped half a block ahead, in the darkest stretch of the side street and three men had climbed down from the driver's cab. Even as she watched, the steel grating at the rear was jerked open. Lights from the far corner made grotesque silhouettes of prisoners and captors and Nita saw a man's arm swing high, glimpsed a whip in his fist! The thud of the whip and the pitiful wail that answered its fall wrung her heart.

"So they're police," Wentworth said softly. His lean hands, catching up two of the automatics from the seat, moved with a swift sureness of long practice. "Stay here, sweet," he ordered. "There are only three of them."

Before Nita could protest, Wentworth was striding swiftly along the asphalt of the street toward the truck. He moved in the shadow of parked cars, but his eyes could comb the fringes of that huddle of men's bodies spilling from the ambulance. His nostrils thinned with anger. He could catch the swift thudding of the whip and the frantic piping shrillness of pain and terror in human voices. One of the prisoners was clinging to the

4

hand grips beside the ambulance door, clinging with hunched shoulders and cringing neck, under the blows of a whip. And his legs… his legs were twisted and wasted beneath him. He was a cripple!

For an instant, between two parked cars, Wentworth could glimpse the whole group, and amazement mingled with his fury, held him motionless in the shadows of the street. Every member of that prisoned group, except those that wielded the whips, was a cripple! They huddled, on helpless legs, or cringed off into the darkness with hunched and twisted backs, fleeing from the whips… Cripples. *Crippled beggars!*

Indignation coursed hotly through Wentworth's veins, while his mind raced to an explanation of this fantastic scene.

This flood of crippled beggars he had seen upon New York's streets, soliciting alms from the hundreds of thousands of visitors who were trooping to the city for the World's Fair, could it be that these beggars were enslaved? That they worked for a single master under the stinging urge of slave whips? Wentworth was remembering the assault of those three cripples upon a citizen, remembering, too, that his friend, Stanley Kirkpatrick, commissioner of police, had told him there had been dozens of foot-pad robberies recently. It was true, there had been no specific mention of cripples, but Wentworth was wondering now if these apparently sporadic outbreaks were not possibly all part of the plan of one man… a slave master of cripples!

Wentworth weighed his automatics in his hands… and stepped abruptly clear of the parked cars.

"That will do," he ordered quietly. "Stand just as you are!"

The three men with whips whirled toward him. Cripples scuttled off into the darkness and the man who clung to the door-handle with cringing powerful shoulders turned a white and pain-racked face.

"For God's sake, go, man," the cripple whispered hoarsely. "You cannot help us. Only God can do that!"

One whipman took a slow stride toward Wentworth. "Listen, buddy," he grumbled. "You know what's good for you, you'll shove off and forget all about this."

Wentworth's chiseled lips were unyielding. He had to force out words. "Drop those whips," he ordered sharply.

"Turn around and face that truck. Quickly..." His guns lifted in his hands and the blue steel caught a gleam of light.

"Hey, don't shoot!" The guard who had spoken flung up his hands, let the whip drop to the pavement. Wentworth saw that its lash was darkly stained, and the coldness of his anger shook him.

"Face the truck!" he ordered again and his voice rasped. THE WHIPMEN obeyed in hurried fright and Wentworth gestured his left gun toward the cripple on the step. All the rest had disappeared, though from the darkness it seemed to Wentworth he could catch the plaintive whispering of their voices, the shuffle of crippled limbs upon the pavement. In heaven's name, why did they still remain? Even this sorely beaten man upon the steps had begged him to leave! Wentworth's eyes focused keenly on the man's face.

This square-jawed, wide-browed face was not that of a street beggar. There was power and strength of will there, and now a frantic pleading. "Please go," he was whispering. "Believe me, you cannot help me, help us. You bring us only death and sorrow."

"What madness is this?" Wentworth snapped. "Search those men for guns. We'll see what the police have to say about this business. I don't know how you men have been enslaved, but there is a cure for it! We'll track down this criminal who herds cripples with whips. You don't look like a man who could be easily intimidated. Fight for your freedom, man! Come now, their guns!"

Some emotion Wentworth could not fathom was working in the cripple's face. His limbs were bent grotesquely beneath him, so that he supported himself more by the power of his hand clinging to the handrail than by actually standing. He obeyed Wentworth's order though Wentworth caught the mutter of a threat from one of the whipmen.

At the sound, the cripple's shoulders flinched as under the shock of a whip, but to Wentworth's urging, he hurried. He fished three guns from the pockets of the guards, twisted about again to face Wentworth. He gripped one of the weapons ready in his right fist.

"Won't you go, sir?" he asked, beseechingly.

"Certainly not," Wentworth snapped. "Throw me the guns, and we'll go to the police."

The cripple lifted the confiscated gun, and fired point-blank at Wentworth! And even as he fired, Wentworth caught his whispering words, "I'm sorry, sir. So sorry!"

Incredulous as he was, Wentworth had caught the man's intention an instant before he fired. He flung himself frantically

aside to the cover of the parked automobiles and his own automatic swiveled up in
swift reprisal… but he held his fire. Despite
the attack, he could not bring himself to kill
this sad-faced cripple. There was some deep
mystery here, and there was horror, too. But
there was no time for thought. The cripple

continued to pump bullets at Wentworth! They ploughed up
the soft asphalt within inches of his head and he rolled, dragged
himself under a car.

Bewilderment was still his primary reaction to this madness,
but swiftly he brushed it from his brain. It was a mystery that
would not worry him long if he did not manage to stop this
fusillade! The bullets were biting closer. He could hear the hoarse
shouts of the guards, glimpse them as they scrambled to regain
their revolvers.

"Close in on him!" That would be the leader of the whipmen.
"Set the car on fire. If he gets away, you'll suffer the penalty, every
one of you. *The full penalty!*"

There were whimpers from the darkness, but even while they
wailed out their fear… the cripples were closing in upon Wentworth. He caught a vibration of sound through the car, of metal
rasping on metal. Good Lord, were they really going to fire
the gas tank? Wentworth twisted and threw a bullet scorching
along the pavement, not to injure, but to warn the cripple there.
He still could not bring himself to fire on these maimed men.
A new hammer of guns blasted through the night. Was it the
guards… *or was it Nita?*

FRANTIC FEAR for her stabbed through Wentworth. There was a flare of light behind him… God, the fool had struck a match. Wentworth pumped a shot directly at the burning match and heard a man scream. Damn it, this was a nightmare thing; cruelly beaten slaves fighting against being given their freedom! Grim-mouthed, Wentworth deliberately stretched his automatics out before him. He could glimpse the legs of men as they spread out to reach him with their bullets… and knew they must be the guards, for these legs were not crippled! Deliberately, Wentworth opened fire.

His first bullet punched a man's leg out from under him and slammed him facedown in the street, and his second shot was flying on its way even before the man hit. There was deadly accuracy in Wentworth's guns, an ability that came from daily practice throughout the years—and scores of battles in which his life had hung utterly on those same accurate automatics. A half-dozen swift shots and the guards were stretched motionless on the pavement.

"Your guards are finished," Wentworth called clearly. "Stop this madness. I don't want to shoot you, but if you continue to attack, I will. Do you hear me, your masters are finished! Dead!"

Behind Wentworth, another match flared into brilliance. With a curse, he thrust himself out from beneath the car while his ready guns weaved in his hands. No shot was hurled toward him, and he glimpsed the pointed, thin face of the cripple who crouched over the mouth of the open gas tank, a burning match in his hand. Even as Wentworth flung up a desperate automatic, the man popped the match out of sight… into the gas tank!

Wentworth had time for one long bounding leap toward the ambulance. He was pitching toward the pavement in a headlong dive when the gasoline tank let go. Flames of yellow and white and crimson fanned out behind the car, threw bloody spikes high into the night. Two bodies heaved, twisting, through the air and a clear high scream sliced through the fury of the blast. The car itself leaped under the spur of the blast, slewed sideways. Flame washed across its top, dripped from its fenders. Gouts of liquid fire spewed over the street. The whole area danced with writhing black shadows from the flicker of a hundred small blazes.

The gust caught Wentworth in mid air, swept past him with a sense of intolerable heat. He hit rolling, crushed out a spear of heat that had stabbed between his shoulders; staggered to his feet. Men's cries drummed on his deafened ear-drums. Two twisted figures that had been cripples were motionless in the street under the lick of the billowing flames that were devouring them. They had caught the full force of the blast and for them there was no help at all.

Wentworth stared toward where he had left the Hispano and the headlights flashed out from it suddenly. It rolled toward him... and he breathed a deep sigh of relief. Nita, then, had avoided the blast. He reached the rear of the ambulance in a bound. A crumpling body still clung by a locked hand to the hand-rail, but flames eddied and leaped around him in a savage torture dance. The man's face was twisted with pain, but there was a beatific smile in his eyes. It was as if, even by this fierce torment, he welcomed death!

Wentworth was ripping off his own coat. He flung it around the tortured body, smothering the flames.

"Mercy, sir," the man gasped. "Let me die. There is no other release."

"Fool!" Wentworth snapped. "You're out of it all right, but there are others who aren't. For their sake, tell me… where will I find the man who enslaved you!"

The man smiled, though his muscles writhed and contorted in pain. He did not speak.

"For the sake of those you love, man," Wentworth said. "Quickly. Tell me, before it's too late."

The man's eyes fixed on his in fierce longing, in greater pain. "Those I love…" he whispered. "Yes, yes, if it is not too late. Listen, man. Garage… Twenty-fourth and…" He shuddered, and his head sagged forward. Wentworth bent over him in desperate haste, but life had left the tortured shell.

SLOWLY, WENTWORTH straightened. The light of the flames was more brilliant. The tires of three cars were blazing where they stood in pools of liquid flame. Within moments, the tanks might let go, and distantly he heard the wail of a fire siren begin. His Hispano jerked to a halt beside him, Nita behind the wheel.

"Hurry, Dick," she cried.

Wentworth nodded stiffly, but before he turned to the car, he sprang toward the body of one of the dead guards and from his pocket he whipped a slim platinum cigarette case.

"No, Dick. *No!*" Nita cried. "The police are on the way. There isn't time!"

11

Gouts of liquid fire spewed over the street after the fury of the blast.

Wentworth made no answer. He bent over the man and ground the base of the lighter against the dead flesh of the forehead. Only an instant he crouched there, his face grim and cold in the flicker of the flames, then he sprang to the running board and the Hispano now leaped forward.

Behind him, the weird light of the fires spilled across the dead face of the man over whom he had bent, and touched the crimson seal that Wentworth had printed on his forehead, a thing of hairy legs and poison fangs, menacing in its silent challenge— *the seal of the Spider!*

It was a deadly dangerous thing that Wentworth had done, but in his face was no recognition of that fact, only grim determination. The glint of his gray-blue eyes was like glacial ice but he relaxed against the cushions of the car while Nita sent it raving through the gear-shifts, darting for the corner. Once they turned that... But Wentworth was thinking of the mission that lay ahead of him, a self-imposed mission, as were all the crusades of this man who used the seal of the Spider. He had just now used that seal with deliberation—in full recognition of the danger it implied—as a warning to the criminal who was behind this horror.

Throughout the length and breadth of the underworld, that seal and the man who had imprinted it were known... and terribly feared. Not that they knew Richard Wentworth to be the Spider. That was a closely guarded secret known only to the woman he loved and a few intimates, for to be revealed as the Spider meant being betrayed to death! Scores of times, that signature of death had been imprinted upon the foreheads of criminals who richly merited their punishment. And so the underworld hunted endlessly for this grim nemesis of the night—as did the law. Much as the police might revere this lone wolf of justice who used the seal, they could regard him only as a man who violated the laws they were sworn to uphold.

Yes, the hunt would be on again but that thought barely crossed Wentworth's mind. Long ago, he had pledged himself to ceaseless battle against the criminals who oppressed and preyed upon mankind. For a while he had worked within the law, but the hampering restrictions, which must be enforced to guard the innocent, had been twisted to their own defense by vicious criminals. The courts were their plaything and the police were helpless to gather evidence where terror strangled their witnesses.

And so, the Spider had been born, to work his bitter vengeance in the night, secretly and alone, and in peril from police and underworld alike....

Now, the Spider must walk again, to scotch this horror that was burgeoning. It was not alone the enslavement of the cripples. There was a deeper, more awful mystery here. Men did not murder, they did not willingly die, to protect a mere beggar's racket. Wentworth knew that he had stumbled on the least out-thrust tentacle of some new and loathsome underworld menace. He knew, without any question, that unless he struck swiftly and surely this master of loathsome slaves would sweep on to a conquest whose echoes would terrify the very nation.

The shriek of a police siren pulled Wentworth's eyes sharply ahead and he saw a radio patrol car rocket around the corner and slam toward him, coming the wrong way on the street. It slewed to a halt, and two men with revolvers in their hands blocked the escape of the Hispano… And behind him, there by the burning cars, the seal of the Spider glimmered upon a dead man's forehead!

CHAPTER 2
THE SPIDER'S WAY

FOR A moment, defeat and capture stared Wentworth in the face. It was true that he had powerful friends, but even his close acquaintance with Commissioner Kirkpatrick would avail him nothing at all if proof that he was the Spider were produced. Kirkpatrick was a man of unflinching duty and stern resolve. It might be possible to talk his way out of this difficulty, but valuable time would be lost. So far, he had not been identified… and he did not intend that he should be!

"Race the motor," he said softly to Nita, "then duck low."

His hand moved like the flick of a whiplash and the dazzling beam of the headlights smote the policemen like a blast of flame. They stumbled, threw up their arms and the roar of the powerful Hispano hammered at them. With hoarse shouts, they hurled themselves from what seemed the path of sure destruction. The instant they were out of the way, Nita let the clutch jump in and the roadster leaped like a racehorse from the barrier. Two, three aching seconds dragged past while the car sprinted for the corner. A single gun-shot blasted out, but Wentworth did not even hear the whine of lead, then the Hispano had whirled the corner and was streaking southward.

Traffic was heavy on Eighth Avenue, for it was the after-the-ater hour and taxis battled with sleek limousines for position. Wentworth had a sharp frown on his forehead as he watched the back-trail. Those police would find it impossible to turn their car in the narrow space between the close parked cars. He thought it likely their eyes had been dazzled by the headlights before they could recognize the car, but the danger was far from past. The Hispano was conspicuous and he was wearing formal evening dress… without a coat!

Wentworth could not delay on that account. Already, the garage on Twenty fourth Street, mentioned by the dying crip-ple, must have been warned of the attack which had wiped out the guards.

"Turn left, Nita," he said softly, "then you'd better take a taxi for home. My home. There's some new warfare breeding, and I can't be sure whether we've been identified."

Nita started a protest even as she whirled the car off Eighth Avenue. "But, Dick, there's no more risk with the two of us in the Hispano than alone. Why not head straight for home now? You can hide the car, and…."

Wentworth's hand closed gently on her arm, "There's work tonight, dear," he said softly. "Work for… the Spider."

Nita caught her breath and her deep violet eyes turned toward him, pleading with words she could never utter. She would never seek to swerve him from the path of duty he had chosen, but always when he went on these mad, single-handed battles against the mighty of the underworld, her heart must be torn with pain.

"Let me go with you, Dick," she urged. "You may need help, and…"

Wentworth shook his head. "It is too dangerous to you, dear. And I must be able to concentrate every effort on the work ahead. With you near, my sweet, it's hard to concentrate on anything else."

Nita moved her hand impatiently. "You're putting me off, Dick."

"No time to waste, dear. Get a taxi at once," he said.

Nita's firm round chin set rebelliously and she tossed her chestnut curls… but she slid out from behind the wheel and stepped to the pavement.

"Be careful, Dick."

Wentworth's smile relaxed the grim set of his jaw and his gray-blue eyes softened. "For your sake, dear," he whispered.

Then he slid the car into gear and sent it humming up the cross-street. In the rear-vision mirror, he saw Nita cross to a taxi at the curb and nodded in satisfaction to himself before he settled to the grim work ahead. He slipped down low in the seat for maximum concealment and shuttled swiftly through cross-town traffic until the dark, deserted streets of the East Side gave him protection.

On a narrow alley where warehouse walls raised their blank surfaces, he checked the Hispano beside the entrance to a private garage. Swiftly, he backed out a battered coupé whose engine sang a sweet song of power, garaged the Hispano in its place…

and stayed inside. He knelt upon the concrete floor and, with a knife blade, prodded at regular intervals along a crease in the cement. There was a click of a released spring and the block of cement hinged upward.

From the cavity under it, Wentworth whipped out a long black cape, a black slouch hat. Beneath it was a neat makeup tray and a wig of dark, lank hair. Deft hands set to work upon his face. A quick smearing of liquid sallowed the skin and drew it tautly across cheek and nasal bones; the lips vanished so that his mouth was a sinister gash and putty formed the nose into a predatory beak. The wig settled into place and, over his smooth brows, he attached bushy clumps of frowning hair. That was all... but the face that peered back at him from the make-up mirror was a vastly different countenance from that of the cultured and wealthy Richard Wentworth. It was sinister, menacing... the face of the Spider!

Wentworth did not linger long over his disguise. Within five minutes of his entrance into the garage, he was behind the wheel of the battered old coupé with its masked, powerful motor, and was once more speeding southward through the city. Twenty-fourth Street... a garage. It would want some finding, but he would succeed. And when he did, there would be a showdown with this whip master of crippled slaves!

THE GARAGE was a forbidding dark building of brick in a block of small shuttered stores. Tenements reared their dreary fire-escape scarred fronts across the street and the dim red light above the driveway was the only sign of life in all that stretch. The only sign until a twisted, hobbling figure flung itself from the shadows and scrambled, groaning for breath, into the driveway. For an instant then, lights flashed brilliantly, to die as quickly as they had bloomed.

"I gotta see the Wreck," the cripple gabbled. "I gotta right away."

The guard at the foot of the auto elevator slipped a hand beneath his cloak and brought it out with a short-handled, many lashed knout in his fist. "You sure you gotta see him, guy?" he asked softly.

The cripple cringed away from the whip and his eyes, bright in a dirty, pinched face, clung to the gaze of the guard. "Honest, I gotta, Mugsy."

The guard called Mugsy grinned with thick lips. "Okay," he agreed softly. "Only if the Wreck don't think it's important, it's going to be too bad." He swung the whip and the knouts cracked against the brick wall.

"I ain't afraid," the cripple mumbled and swung himself on his one crutch into the elevator.

He licked his lips with a furtive tongue and glanced about warily, as if he expected torture to spring at him from the brick walls of the shaft. The elevator heaved itself upward heavily and it was on the top floor that the guard flung down the barrier gate. The cripple's crutch tapped across the concrete floor; his breath was noisy. The office in the corner of the floor was brick-walled and the door was solid, but beneath it a sliver of light stole out, secretively.

"You wait here," the guard ordered and rapped in a peculiar

cadence on the heavy door. Afterward, he opened it and went inside. When he gestured the cripple into the lighted room, the man pulled off his dog-eared hat and fumbled it against his chest. He went into the room meekly.

There was a single window in the office, and a brilliant overhead light that threw the heavy desk and the man behind it into deep shadow. Gleams of it caught in his eyes, which were enormous under cavernous brows, and made them glisten strangely. His shoulders were hunched so that his head seemed to start forward from between them, and his hands, thick with black hair, moved restlessly across the top of the desk.

"Well, slave?" he said softly.

The cripple stuttered in an effort to get out words fast. "Geez, Wreck," he said humbly, "don't go scaring me like that. I got news. It ain't good news, but it's important. I swear it is. Maybe you wouldn't want Mugsy to hear." He waited.

"Maybe," said the man addressed as the Wreck.

The whip guard grinned and strode toward the door. As he went through, the lashes snapped against the brick wall and the cripple hunched his shoulders, shivering.

"Look, Wreck," he mumbled. "I was in the dog wagon, you know, and up on Forty-eighth Street, we was being unloaded, when a guy comes up and starts shooting. He bumped your three whips. We tried to pull him down. Geez, Marbles even tossed a match into a gas tank. It got him, but it didn't get this guy. And look, when he went away, he put something red on the forehead of one of your whips. It was a red spider."

The Wreck exploded an oath, hoarsely. "The Spider!"

The cripple shivered and backed toward the door. "I hurried right back to tell you, Wreck. One of us—you know the big guy you call Doc. Well, he told the Spider something just before he died of the fire. I don't know what it was, but maybe…."

"Yes, maybe." The Wreck's voice was soft again. "You have done me a service, small broken worm. For that, you shall have a day off and a double ration."

The cripple's face brightened in a wide smile. "Oh, Geez, Wreck. Thank you!"

"But," the Wreck went on, "you left your post of duty, and for that there shall be a small penalty. Just a small penalty."

The cripple dropped his crutch and thumped down on his one knee. He shrieked, and the entrance of Mugsy made him grovel.

"Caress him three times, Mugsy," said the Wreck.

The knout whistled and thudded, and afterward the guard hauled the unconscious cripple out of the office where the monster who called himself the Wreck crouched, waiting like a hungry beast. When Mugsy came back, the Wreck was smiling so that his rotted stumps of teeth showed brokenly.

"We shall need the boys in the basement, Mugsy," he said, in the same gentle tones. "A gentleman is going to call on us and I want everything prepared. Every door is to be sealed tightly. We will arrange things so that the gentleman must enter by this window whose light will tell him many… misleading things. The trap we arranged here will not go unused, Mugsy."

The ferret eyes of the whip guard swung toward the window, then glanced toward the two walls and an awed smile touched his mouth. "Gawd, Wreck," he whispered, "you think of every-thing."

"And I remember those who serve me well," the Wreck replied. "Or not so well!"

Mugsy's smile pinched off his mouth as he ducked out of the door and his feet beat hurriedly across the concrete of the floor. The Wreck's body did not move, but his long-fingered hand slid open a drawer and lingered over a series of electric buttons there. The smile broadened on his mouth.

"You do well, my Wreck," he whispered to himself. "Yes, very well. Shall we not find a way to make this same Spider serve us? Many men and women serve us well, and dare not do other-wise. Why not this same gentleman, the Spider? He chuckled and the laughter shook him. His great, bushy head wobbled on a stalk of a neck and his arched shoulders wrenched. He gasped with the thought of it. "Yes, yes, the Spider shall serve me, too."

Presently, men filed into the room—four of them besides Mugsy, and all had the subdued aspect of terror. They kept their eyes on the Wreck as caged birds might watch an approaching and deadly serpent.

"I shall have work for you presently, gentlemen," the Wreck said. "We are going to prepare a welcome for a guest. Afterward, we shall have a certain task to perform. I find that my supply of cripples is becoming exhausted. We shall have to make some more. I hope I make myself clear? Yes, yes, I see that I do. Those who serve me well do not become… cripples. Now, may I have your full attention, gentlemen?"

IN ALL, there were seven garages scattered along the length of Twenty fourth Street between the Hudson River and the East River. Wentworth had started on the western end, had completed the search, but still he was not certain. There was nothing to choose among the places—no way to say definitely that one was the place in which the slave-master of the cripples had his headquarters.

That was the first time he coasted along the dark stretch of the street, but the second time he checked his car sharply close to the corner. He had seen a twisted, crippled man dart from the shadowed doorway of the gaunt building half-way down the street. He was visible only an instant before the shadows swallowed him beyond the blood-red pool of the single light that burned there.

Slowly, the keen eyes of the Spider swept the face of the building. It was dark, sealed tight… except that high up on the topmost floor there was a lighted window. Wentworth made a swift estimate and nodded slightly to himself. Easy to reach

RICHARD WENTWORTH

that window by climbing to the roof of the adjoining tenement building. He could see the web-like tracery of a fire-escape ladder mounting to the garage roof. From there to the window sill the climb would be very easy!

Wentworth parked the coupé and merged his long, caped body into the shadows. There was no sound of footfalls on the quiet of the street, no trace at all of the Spider's passage save that now and then a shadow seemed to swell and move. The dark-

25

ened doorway of a tenement building received him and he went soundlessly up stairs that would shriek aloud to casual passage; emerged presently on the roof. Moments later, he was testing the fire-escape ladder, and estimating more closely the span to the window sill. He nodded. It was easy....

Briefly, his hands brushed the butts of the twin automatics holstered beneath his arms. They were fully loaded, a bullet in the chamber. The lipless gash of the Spider's mouth was cold with menace. He did not know what riddle would be solved here, but he knew that the man who proclaimed himself master of these crippled slaves warranted death. It was a warrant the Spider would take it on himself to solve!

Swiftly then, he mounted the ladder and reached across the blank expanse of the wall to the lighted window. His fingers clamped around an awning rod and he drew himself across the gap. Now, he could catch the hoarse rumble of men's voices; could catch the precise accents of one that was hissingly gentle in tone, yet cold with cruelty. The Spider's eyes narrowed and he bent closer to distinguish precise words.

"Those who serve me well," the voice was saying, "do not become... cripples. Now, may I have your full attention, gentlemen?"

Wentworth risked a quick glance into the room, saw that five men were huddled about the single doorway and that another, misshapen figure hunched behind the desk. It was the man behind the desk who was talking.

"Not only has the number of my slaves been reduced tonight," he said softly, "but for the bigger plans, for which I have been training them, I shall need a great many more. Say, five hundred. However, for tonight, a mere fifty will serve my purposes very well. Of course, I do not expect you to create these cripples for me. That is a task beyond your skill, but you can snare for me the specimens I need. My skill will serve—if you bring me healthy specimens. The old ones and the feeble ones, you will kill."

Outside the window, Wentworth felt the coldness of his anger seep through his veins. If he understood this creature inside, the fiend was proposing to kidnap men and make cripples of them, to twist their bodies with tortures into inhuman shapes, to enslave them by what process God alone knew.

Coolly, Wentworth made his plans. He drew one automatic from its holster, and tensed his muscles. A blow would shatter the glass and send him bounding through into the office. Thereafter, his guns would give him ample protection. Fierce exultation was in his breast. He was striking in time… in time to save fifty human beings from death, and worse… to save them from the tortures of this mass murderer.

"It will be simple enough if you follow my plans," the man was saying, "the buses that are coming into the city hourly are loaded to the bumpers with fine healthy specimens, bound for the World's Fair and a holiday." The man chuckled, and his arched shoulders jerked with the laughter. "Well, we will give them a longer holiday than they reckon for! It is simple to divert a bus from its course. You men will find bus driver uniforms provided for you. You will stop and enter these buses and… well, *relieve* the drivers. Afterward, you will know where to drive the buses and the specimens. That will be all, gentlemen!"

WENTWORTH SUCKED in a slow breath. If he waited for the men to leave, he would reduce the odds against him tremendously… but also he would release them to carry out the ferocious orders of this monster. It was a choice over which many men might have hesitated, but for the Spider there could be no hesitation. He loosened his taut muscles, drove in the window-pane with a crooked knee and hurled himself into the room!

Men whipped toward him and their hands flew toward armpit guns, but Wentworth's two automatics were in his fists.

"Don't move, gentlemen," he said, in mocking imitation of the leader's tones. "If you do, I'm afraid some of you may be crippled… by my bullets. *The Spider orders you!*"

Under the lowered brim of his black hat, his eyes were every-where. He saw that the man behind the desk had his hand in an open drawer, but before he could lift and level a weapon, the Spider's swift guns could smash the life from him. Wentworth wanted him to try that. He did not kill even such criminals as this creature, in cold blood, unarmed and defenseless. None of the five crooks at the door moved, and Wentworth straightened slightly from his fighting crouch.

"Turn around and face the wall," he ordered sharply.

White-faced, the men started to obey and then, behind him, Wentworth heard a slight rasp of metal on metal. With an oath, he hurled himself backward so that his shoulders brought up against the wall beside the window. Had he walked into a trap? Was someone coming up behind him, to attack?

"Don't move," he snapped again at the six men before him, on whom his guns still bore.

28

He risked a short glance toward the window, and surprise put a crease between the heavy brows of the Spider. There was no menace there, but he no longer had a lane of retreat open. A solid sheet of steel closed the window.

Wentworth laughed shortly. Did they think to trap him by closing the way back? He had no intention of retreat—while his prey still lay before him. His eyes whipped back to the six men and he saw them move. The gun in his right hand spat flame and lead, and the pain of concussion drove in on his ear-drums. The man did not fall, but in the clear air before him suddenly there was a curious hallucination. There seemed to be a silvery star there in the air which caught glints of light from the overhead globe. And the men made no attempt to pull their guns. They were grinning....

An oath leapt to Wentworth's lips as he realized the nature of the trap into which he had sprung. The window behind him was sealed impregnably and in that brief instant, while he had turned toward the sound, a veil had been drawn across the room—a veil which gave a curious greenish cast to the faces of the men beyond it, and in which the silvery star of the bullet scar stood out. He knew in that same instant what this veil was... a screen of bullet-proof glass!

Even as he recognized that fact, he sent his eyes questing over the screen, but it sealed him in from wall to wall, from floor to ceiling. And the man behind the desk had swiveled in his chair, his vicious grin showing the rotting stumps of his teeth.

"You see, gentlemen," he was saying softly, and the voice came to Wentworth's ears with a curious vibration as if it were mechanically transmitted. "You see, I was right in installing this little trap. We have caught a spider. I think he will make a very useful slave... after we have crippled him a little."

Wentworth stared at the man with dawning horror; not at the thing that had been threatened against himself but with the sudden full knowledge of what this man was doing to the city. He was remembering that even before the opening of the World's Fair, the lists of missing persons had taken a tremendous leap upward, and now he understood the answer. This hideous creature had seized them and turned them into human monsters to do his bidding.

Furiously, Wentworth started forward, his guns ready in his fists. He must break through this trap somehow, prevent this man from going upon his vicious errand. They could not kill him without opening at least a loop-hole in the glass, and when they did....

"Mugsy," the leader was saying. "I leave you in charge of our guest. Unfortunately, he will find himself a bit close in his room. There is no way for air to enter it, so in a matter of hours, he will begin to suffocate. When he has quite succumbed, you may chain him up to await my pleasure. Now, gentlemen, on your way. Fifty strong slaves, gentlemen, will satisfy me for the present. Fifty slaves who can stand a bit of crippling..." He laughed. Then he tossed up his heavy, misshapen head and the long, hairy fingers clutched into fists.

"Spider," he gasped. "I leave you to your meditations."

He hobbled across the room and flung a black cape not unlike the Spider's own about his shoulders, dragged on a soft felt hat.

"Meditate well, Spider," he said. "I shall have need of your fine brain presently... when you have been properly crippled. Yes... yes. Well, good night."

He sauntered out through the door and all of the men save only one followed him.

Wentworth stood motionless in the midst of his sealed and air-tight chamber and his guns hung heavy in his hands. The reek of cordite was strangling in his nostrils, and already the air was close. Trapped... Neatly and hopelessly trapped, and this creature was going out to kidnap and to maim!

CHAPTER 3
NITA DISOBEYS

I T WAS not often that Nita van Sloan disregarded the orders that Richard Wentworth gave her in time of stress. Not that he was an unreasonable or arbitrary lover, but when the Spider went upon his forays against the lawless, his home and his associates operated on a military basis. It had to be that way, for when the Spider went upon a hunt... Death hunted him! Yet this night, when Nita saw the swift Hispano leap from her side, she felt an overpowering fear. There had been no time to persuade Dick. Indeed, there had been no grounds on which to argue... and yet, the feeling persisted... fear for the man she loved.

Consequently, when she entered the taxi, she said quietly, "Follow that roadster ahead, and don't lose sight of it."

While Wentworth was putting on his disguise in the garage,

Nita raced the taxi to a concern where she could rent a car to drive herself. She returned just in time to pick up the trail to the garage on Twenty-fourth Street and the minutes that followed the Spider's disappearance into the shadows seemed hours long. She clutched in both hands one of the automatics from the Hispano. She waited.

Her fear-sharpened eyes saw Wentworth's shadowy figure scale the wall, and saw his leap into the lighted room… and afterward she saw that light blotted out and the echo of a single shot came faintly to her ears. Nita sat tensely forward and her hands were white with the strain of her grip upon the automatic. There was no farther sound; no hint of what might be happening within that gaunt dead building. One shot… Dear God, who had fired it, and what had that single hurtling bullet done?

Nita found herself on the pavement beside her rented car. Everything in her urged an immediate frontal attack upon the garage, but sanity and experience told her that was madness. If Dick had failed… Swiftly, Nita pivoted and ran along the empty street toward where pale light filtered out through the grease-filmed windows of an all-night restaurant.

There was a pay phone on the wall and she went to it without a glance for the two men seated at the counter, ignoring their boldly appraising stare. Nita had no fear of them, though, she knew her fragile provocative dress, the velvet cloak about her shoulders, had set them whispering. Her right hand, under the fold of her cloak, held a heavy automatic competently. She was more accustomed to a .38, but she could manage a .45, too, thanks to Dick's long training.

Swiftly, she put through a call to Went-
worth's fortress home and summoned Jack-
son to the phone—Jackson whose official
title was chauffeur but who had fought side
by side with the Spider through many a
bitter battle against the underworld. She
spoke in slow and careful French so that he
could understand… and the men in the restaurant could not.

"The master is in danger!" she said. "A new warfare. I think
he has been taken prisoner. Bring the Sikh at once to Twenty-fourth and First. I will meet you there. And hurry. Hurry!"

There was a steady competence in Nita's manner, complex
absence of apprehension that prevented even a whispered over-
ture from the men in the restaurant as she hurried out again.
She gave them no thought and tried rapidly to form some plan
of action. With Jackson and Wentworth's body servant, the
doughty Sikh, Ram Singh, behind her, she would have a fighting force equal to almost any emergency.

From her seat in the rented car, she studied the garage… and
kept a watch for the arrival of her allies. Still no sound, no gleam
of light from the garage; only that blood-red exit lamp, ominous
as a leering eye. The distant rumble of an elevated train, softened on the warm night air, only made the silence more deep.…

AND THEN noisily, the garage doors racketed up into their
slot and a car glided down the ramp. For an instant, it was
silhouetted brilliantly against the driveway lights and Nita's
heart leaped sickeningly, began to thud heavily against her
breast. Inside that car was a hunched figure wearing a cape

and a black slouch hat. Dick! It had to be Dick. No other man assumed such a disguise. He was a prisoner, as she had feared, and Jackson had not come!

Nita drew in a shuddering breath. Only one thing to do. She must follow the criminal car and hope against hope that her one gun would be enough. If she had an opportunity, she could call Wentworth's aged butler, Jenkyns, and leave a farther message for Jackson and Ram Singh. They would be sure to call back for instructions when they failed to find her. All was not yet lost.

As soon as the car ahead turned the corner, Nita started her small coupé and shot it forward on the parallel street, paused at the next intersection to make sure that she had taken the right course. The limousine shot past and once more she saw the silhouette of that hunched, caped figure. She nodded, touched the gun on the seat beside her, and pushed on northward. There was a bare chance that she might meet Jackson and Ram Singh on the way. But even if she didn't… Nita's round chin set firmly and her soft lips were compressed. They would find that the Spider's mate could be deadly, too!

The pursuit passed within a few blocks of Wentworth's fortress home, built mostly on filled land between two East River piers, and Nita felt an almost terrible temptation to turn aside and seek help there. She dared not lose sight of the limousine in which she was sure Dick was being held prisoner. She must be close enough, if they acted against him, to strike with all the strength she possessed. Suppose they simply shot him in the car, as criminals had been known to do, before this, with their prisoners? For a wild moment, Nita was goaded to drive her light coupé into a crash with the limousine. If she fired rapidly, and with the sure accuracy Dick had drilled into her hands....

Yes, in extremity, she would do precisely that, but her chances of success would be slight and she was Dick's only hope! She schooled herself to patience and dodged back and forth across the trail of the limousine while it sped steadily northward, crossing through Harlem into the Bronx; droning on without pause or delay. It left the brighter thoroughfares then, swung eastward, and at long last, it paused before the broad doorways of a warehouse. Nita had turned the corner and it was too late to check her approach, so she drove straight on at a steady pace. Only, when she passed the doors, she risked a quick glance into the warehouse entrance.

The hunched, caped figure of a man had scrambled out of the car and yellow light reached in under the brim of his hat as he stared toward the passing car. Nita gasped... and stepped sharply on the accelerator. She had been tricked, *tricked!* Even in disguise, Wentworth could not achieve that horrid face and the hunch of the shoulders, the predatory forward thrust of the head was menacing, awful.

Oh, what could have happened to Dick back there in that drab garage on Twenty fourth Street that this monster had stolen his robes! She had been led miles away from where Dick was, at best, imprisoned. Her hands gripped the wheel desperately and she sent the coupé looping around a corner, ground the accelerator to the floor.

She realized now that it had been madness to put on sudden speed this way. They would be after her, and this engine would be no match for the hurricane speed of the heavy car of the criminals. Even as the thought crossed her mind, dazzling headlights slashed the night, threw the spindling shadow of her own car before her. Above the laboring of her own engine, she could hear the booming thunder of a powerful motor. No chance to distance that other car in a straight-away. She could only dodge and twist.

Nita whipped the wheel hard over and stood on the brakes, took a skidding turn into a side street at better than fifty miles an hour; heard the shriek of other brakes as the other machine prepared to follow. And then it happened. Into the opposite end of the street skidded another machine. In an instant, it had twisted broadside across the street and men with guns in their fists were spreading out behind it. She was trapped!

Grimly, Nita trod on the accelerator and headed for the narrow gap of the sidewalk. Gun-flame lanced at her from the darkness ahead and the steering-wheel wrenched wildly under her hands as the bullet tore off a tire. She whipped the car to a standstill, left the lights blazing to blind the marksmen ahead and scrambled to the pavement, gun in hand. If she could reach one of the flanking buildings, she might stand a chance.

She kicked off her high heel slippers and ran. The cloak fluttered out from her shoulders like another Spider's cape, a challenge like a flaunting battle flag. Headlights made an almost tangible wall of dazzling whiteness, limned her lithe woman's figure, a perfect target. Nita's head was wrenched backward, her teeth set on her full lower lip. There was a narrow doorway in the blank warehouse wall ahead. If she could reach that... Strangely, the men were holding their fire.

Through the stillness, broken only by the soft thud of her feet, she heard a man's whispering, piercing voice. She knew that it was the voice of that monster.

"Take her quickly, but alive. Hurry, gentlemen. The bus will be here soon."

Nita's breath pushed out in a sob. Alive... The memory of that hunched monster and his awful face loomed before her, more horrid than death. But alive, she might still help Dick. She might... Nita flung herself at the niche in the wall. The door... was locked! Her automatic spouted at the lock, but the whole barrier was steel. Not a chance. She whirled, her woman's soft shoulders set against the steel, the heavy automatic dwarfing her slim white hand. Her breast lifted in quick, straining breaths. She was ready, the Spider's mate....

"I warned you, gentlemen," that aching whisper came again. "The bus is due... *Hurry!*"

One of the cars began to move toward her. Nita lifted her automatic....

TRIP NUMBER Three of the Down East Bus Company was in two sections and now, near the end of their long run to New York, bearing their quota of crowds for the World's Fair, the two big buses were running close together. The somnolent passengers swayed in their seats. Jim White, the driver hunched in relaxed ease over the wheel, spotting one by one the familiar landmarks stringing along the road.

In the Bronx now. Another three quarters of an hour and he'd roll her into the terminal, then a quick check-up and home. Mary would be waiting up for him like she always did. Jim grinned a little, thinking of Mary, his square hands easy on the great, stubborn wheel. She didn't need a map any longer to follow his path down. She'd be pretty sure that right now he was making this turn off the Post Road. A swell kid, Mary....

Jim threw a quick glance into the rear vision mirror. That girl in Seat Twelve was a lot like Mary with her black crisp hair and her wide-awake blue eyes. *She* wasn't sleeping. Behaving like she'd never taken a bus trip before, staring out the window, sitting tense and excited....

Jim lifted his voice. "In New York now, folks," he drawled. "Won't be long!"

"Relieve the drivers," the Wreck had said. *"You will know where to drive the buses and the specimens. Healthy specimens make good cripples."*

Jim White, the driver, smiled at the way the girl sat up straighter and looked around her more keenly. That guy across the aisle was watching her, too, a smile on his mouth. He'd better not try to get fresh with Twelve... But, shucks, he wouldn't. Bus driving was a sight better than truck hauls. Folks were like a big family. That little old lady back there with the quick bird eyes— she had made the trip a half dozen times with him. Jim knew all about her and her daughter, Lillian, here in New York. Mrs. Markham liked to talk about Lillian. She smiled at Jim in the mirror. Her little paper wrapped package was on her knees, like it had been all the way down. A cake for Lillian….

The Wreck had said, *"The old and feeble ones, you will kill."*

The girl in Twelve turned her head quickly as the man spoke to her across the aisle. "Honest, I don't bite," he said. "Look, I'm a stranger here, too. Just coming down to the Fair. Any reason why you wouldn't talk to me a while? Maybe we could see some of the sights together. Look, I'll tell you about me."

The girl's vivid blue eyes had a sparkle. "Any reason why I should be interested?" she asked coolly.

"I can't think of one," the man grinned. He had a nice, big-toothed smile, and his sandy hair was tousled. "Just say I like to talk about myself. My name's Frank Deacon and I sell automobiles… sometimes. Back in a land's end town called Noank, near the Mystic Isles."

The girl's head swung about quickly, in spite of herself. "Is this a fairy tale?" she asked dryly.

Frank Deacon laughed. "No, that name used to get me, too. They're just a bunch of sand flats, these Mystic Isles, full of clam shells and bad smells."

The girl wrinkled up her nose. "I'm too young to be disillusioned like this," she said, and laughed.

Behind her, old Mrs. Markham leaned forward. "He's a nice boy," she said gently. "You don't need to worry about him."

The girl twisted about in her seat. "I hardly ever worry."

Mrs. Markham smiled. "He has nice hands."

Frank Deacon felt himself flushing, and he laughed. "Here,

here," he said. "I don't go for vivisection like this. Now let's talk about you."

Vivisection....

The Wreck had said, *"I do not expect you to create these cripples for me... snare the specimens. My skill will serve."*

The bus rumbled on through changing traffic lights, speeding southward through the Bronx, toward the terminal... so they all thought. Jim White only frowned a little when he saw two men in bus company uniform signaling him under the street light. He eased on the air and the heavy bus trundled to a stop. The passengers didn't even notice. There had been a lot of red lights.

The girl in Twelve clasped her hands in her lap. "I'm so impatient," she confessed. "Every time the bus stops, I get mad."

Frank Deacon laughed. "Miss Knight, this is going to be fun. We won't have to pretend we aren't excited."

The two men in uniforms were climbing in through the front door. One of them glanced quickly over the bus. His eyes rested for a moment on old Mrs. Markham, lighted when they touched Frank Deacon and the girl. He nodded and turned where the other uniformed man was bending toward the driver.

"What's up?" said Jim White cheerily.

The man bent closer and what he answered was inaudible to the passengers. Presently, Jim White scrambled up from behind the wheel and walked, lurching, toward the door. There was no smile on his white face and Mrs. Markham leaned forward.

"I never saw them change drivers before," she said gently. "It seems a little funny."

Frank Deacon turned, grinning. "Maybe he lives near here and they're giving him a break."

The bus lurched forward somewhat roughly and behind them there was a single sharp blast. The girl, Bonnie Knight, started and uttered a soft cry, "That sounded like a shot," she whispered.

The man in uniform, standing by the driver, spoke flatly. "That was a backfire," he said. "See, a backfire." His eyes flicked over the passengers coldly. Most of them were still drowsing and his gaze centered on the three in the middle who were talking, Frank Deacon and Bonnie and old Mrs. Markham. The old lady smiled at him a little timidly.

She said to Bonnie Knight, "I don't like *his* hands."

FRANK DEACON masked his stare at the man. It seemed unlikely that there was anything wrong happening. Why should anything happen? Yet that sound had been like a shot, and there had been a curious frightened stiffness to the face of the driver when he lurched off the bus. Moreover, there was hostility and menace in the posture and hard eyes of this man in uniform. He kept watch over them like… like a guard.

He felt the bus heel to a fast turn and Mrs. Markham's whisper reached his ear. We don't usually turn here."

As if that hostile, watching man had heard, he said shortly, "Got to stop for gas."

It was then that Frank Deacon knew definitely that something had gone wrong. They had made a gas stop no longer than an hour before! His eyes narrowed speculatively. He thought he could take that man in uniform if he could get close enough to him even if the man were armed. He said, without moving his

The men of the Wreck moved swiftly, and
the prisoners were herded into trucks.

lips. "I'm going up to have a talk with this lad, Bonnie, you and the lady wake up the men as soon as I stand up. Something's wrong!"

He lurched to his feet and stole a glance at the girl. Her eyes were wide and excited. She was a cute kid. He jerked his eyes back to the man in uniform and forced a smile to his mouth.

"I don't think we need any gas," he said quietly. "Maybe you didn't know, but we stopped only an hour ago and filled up." He was only making an excuse for getting close enough to strike. His shoulders felt taut and ready and the muscles in his thighs pulled with every step. "We're pretty anxious to get to the terminal, you know, and finish this trip...."

Two more steps and he could hit. He realized that there was no complete logic in what he was doing, but he *knew* he was right. There was a touch of coldness along his spine. The man's eyes were resting on him sardonically.

"The trip's almost over," the man said.

Frank Deacon took one of those last two steps, and abruptly the uniformed man's hand moved into sight. From his fist there snouted the black and menacing barrel of a revolver. He didn't say anything more. He just stood there, with readiness in his eyes and the brassy smile on his mouth, and the gun jutting from his fist. Frank felt a warm flush sweep over him and afterward he was cold. He had felt the same way once when he had just missed a head-on crash with a truck. It made him angry and his dark eyes grew darker.

"So it's a holdup?" he said loudly. "You can't get away with this. We Ye too many for you."

The gun jerked in the man's fist and Frank found himself flat on his back in the aisle. The blast of it racketed through the bus and there were frightened cries, a panic of sound. Frank tried to hurl himself to his feet, and there was a weakness in his chest that wouldn't let him, and pain began to crawl out of the numbness of his shoulder. He heard the gun smash out again and afterward a woman screamed—a girl, Bonnie….

"Oh, you've killed her," she sobbed. "You've killed the old lady. You… you beast."

The uniformed man spoke again then, softly. "Sit down, babe, or you'll get the same. I ain't going to hurt none of the rest of you, if you sit tight. I got orders not to hurt you." Frank, staring up at him through dizzy eyes, saw the man's teeth briefly between tight lips. "We got other uses for you!"

The bus made two quick, weaving turns and then the exhaust thundered in a confined space before the engine was cut off. Frank Deacon felt a kick drive into his side and, afterward, he was moving, but blindly, without sense of his whereabouts. The pain was spreading downward through his chest, and there was a warm creeping on his flesh that he knew was blood. Dimly, he heard a man's voice.

"Naw, he ain't hurt, boss. I just broke a bone for you. And I got rid of an old dame that wouldn't be no use to us."

A whisper answered him. "Gentlemen, you have done splendidly. These are excellent specimens. Very excellent indeed." Frank Deacon got his eyes open. He was leaning dizzily against the side of the bus and Bonnie Knight was beside him, supporting him. He turned his head heavily. There was a package on the ground by the bus steps, a carefully tied package, crushed and broken by the kicking passage of many feet. Mrs. Markham's cake… Fury welled up in him and such hatred as he had never known before. It cleared his head and he glared at the men that ringed him round, found a misshapen creature who smiled at him wintrily with snarling lips… the Wreck.

"I can see," said the Wreck softly, "that my misshapen body does not please you, my dear fellow. Perhaps, you will have more… sympathy, presently. Yes, yes. Presently…" The crippled man twisted his head about in a quick, reptilian movement. "Get on with your work, gentlemen. Then take these specimens to the place that you know. I will join you. Ah, yes, six culls. When you have finished with them, load them on the buses and take them back on the main route."

The hunched figure in the swirling cape and black slouch hat moved awkwardly across the great warehouse floor where the buses were parked. There were a half-dozen large, enclosed trucks, and huddled groups of people. Frank's eyes fixed on a woman in evening dress who stood with a proudly uplifted head, a torn velvet cloak about her shoulders, and there was pity in the woman's eyes as they rested on him and the girl. Somehow, the sight of her calmed Frank Deacon's fury. She seemed so detached, so contemptuous of the criminals who held them prisoner….

NOTHING OF what she felt showed in her face, but there was grief and a great fear in Nita van Sloan's heart. It was a blow to her pride that she had been captured so easily when the bullet-proof body of the car had crowded her into the doorway a half block from this hideout of the criminals. Yet, it was not for herself that she chiefly suffered. This man who was called, and satirically termed himself the Wreck, had reason actively to hate her, but these others….

Nita flinched at a swift roll of muffled gunfire and her head jerked about. On the floor, six old men and women were writhing out their lives. The 'culls,' the Wreck had called them. Uncontrollably, Nita shuddered. If that was the fate meted out to them, God alone knew what horror awaited herself and these others! God knew what had happened to the man she loved, to Dick....

The men of the Wreck moved swiftly and always their eyes flitted sidewise to where the crippled monster stood and there was fear in their glances. The prisoners were herded together and manacled in pairs, thrust into the big covered trucks. In darkness they huddled against the sides and waited. Nita heard the wounded man whispering to the black-haired girl; a man's voice close beside her repeating broken words endlessly. It was the man whose wrist was handcuffed to her own.

"Now, now, Sarah, nothing will happen to you. I know nothing will happen to you. What could happen, child? Suppose they take our money, does it matter?"

"But, Daddy...."

"Ssh, go to sleep, Sarah. Tomorrow or the next day, we will go to the Fair."

Nita felt her heart swell. What fate lay ahead she could only guess, but that it would be something other than immediate death she surmised from the treatment accorded the "culls" of the Wreck. What was it that horrible cripple had said to the wounded boy? *"You do not like my misshapen body? Perhaps you will have more... sympathy, presently."* There was a hint there of their fate, an indication her mind dare not follow to its logical conclusion!

Nita tried to compose herself, to rest. It was what Dick always did when anxiety and thought would accomplish nothing. The man manacled to her left wrist was singing softly now to the child he called Sarah. His voice was gentle.

Presently, the truck engines began to mutter and they lurched into motion. Hours dragged past while the big vehicles trundled through city streets and afterward went more rapidly on open roads. The close sounds of traffic died away and, occasionally, the engines ground in low gear on hills. They must be far from the city....

Finally, Nita dropped into a troubled sleep haunted by the hunch-backed apparition whom in her own mind she designated as the Monster. When she started awake, it was to find the rear doors of the truck standing open and the early sunlight striking into their close prison.

NITA STAGGERED to her feet and the man handcuffed to her looked up almost timidly, and smiled a little. "I'm afraid it will be awkward for you," he whispered, "but I don't want to wake Sarah."

"No, don't." Nita smiled back at him. She held out her arm so that he could lift and carry the child, and together they moved toward the door. She glanced about her. The wounded boy had a feverish flush in his cheeks and the girl at his side had a stunned, frightened look. In the doorway of the truck, Nita paused.... and horror struck through her like the cold stab of steel.

The place itself was lovely, a sanitarium with great sun decks surrounding a white, plastered house. The sweep of lawn was sweet with fresh grass, but the people scattered about.... Nita shuddered in spite of herself. In wheelchairs, or limping upon crutches, dragging themselves along on roller-fitted platforms, she saw the patients. There were blind men and women who doddered with hunched backs though their faces still held the hints of youth and beauty; there were children without legs, and there were faces from which no human soul gazed forth. Everywhere, they were sprawled upon the grass.... awesome, distorted, crippled human monsters!

There were guards about the trucks with ready guns and a man in a white interne's jacket bustled importantly forward. "Ready for the new patients," he said briskly. "Here's a list of those you are to take back with you. This way, please, everybody—and hurry. The Master is waiting."

He signaled.

Nita fought against the nauseous horror that gripped her throat. She no longer had need to guess at the fate that awaited them. The things she had seen in the last twenty-four hours, the scene before her now, needed no explanation. For a moment, wild rebellion raced through her, but handcuffed as she was, what could she do? Rush away through these green fields? But bullets would find her too swiftly. She strained at the handcuff and the child stirred uneasily in the man's arms. His eyes swung beseechingly to Nita's. With a frantic effort, Nita calmed herself. She could not drag this man with her, and the handcuff kept her from individual flight.

Woodenly, she followed the others as they trooped toward the pleasant facade of the building. A few of the people about her were talking excitedly in hopeful voices, but the others...

well, they had seen the cripples. Consciously, they might not have gauged the thing that was to happen to them, but the dreary sight of the patients weighed upon them. Nita gathered her reserves. At least when the time came to… to do what they intended to do, they would have to free her from this man beside her. When that moment came, she would take her chance!

So Nita thought, but when the moment came, they were all in rooms which had barred windows and iron-grated doors and there was no escape. Frenzy was upon her, the madness of a trapped animal. Her hands clenched at her sides until the nails gouged flesh and, always, her eyes danced about, seeking the way out.…

It did not come and, a half-hour after she had been thrust into a chamber that contained only women, the guards came for her. It was all she could do not to scream and fight with mad hopelessness. Better to relax, to let them think that she suspected nothing. Then, perhaps.…

The two men who gripped her arms never relaxed their hold. They led her through a heavy door that was bolted behind them, and to her nostrils came the sickening sweet scent of ether. It was the final confirmation of the thing she had guessed. She had been brought here to be crippled, to be made into one of those twisted half-human beings with hunched backs or warped limbs.

Nita went a little mad. She struck out at the men who gripped her with all the skill of *jiu-jitsu* that Wentworth had taught her. She flung one of them, reeling, against the wall and saw him slump, half-conscious, to the floor. But before she could whirl, the second man sent his fist crashing against her jaw and for a while she knew no more.

Recovery was leaden and painful. She was strapped motionless to a table and her hands moved against her naked flesh. She rolled her head and saw the brilliant mirrors of a shadowless operating-light over her head; smelled the stronger bite of ether. A face hovered over her, the hateful face of the Monster. Nita shuddered and, in her soul, she said a prayer. If Dick could not come *now*, might he never come! Might she die under the ether. Might she....

Nita choked back the moan that rose to her lips and fought to resurrect the hope that had never died in her before. Always before when she had been captured by his enemies, Dick had managed to find her in time. But he had gone into that garage and there had been that shot... Nita opened her eyes to the laughing sibilance of the Monster.

"No, no, we will not touch her face," he was whispering. "It is much too lovely, and it would have a certain value above a crippled body. We will just do a few things to these lovely legs; perhaps weaken this straight back a trifle... Very well, doctor, the ether. I am quite ready for work."

Sick horror flooded through Nita's soul. She fought frenziedly against the straps that bound her, twisted her head to avoid the ether cone until brutal hands seized her throat and held her motionless. She put her gaze above that monstrous, evil face that hovered over her. Her lips were locked shut, but still as the ether blacked out her senses, her heart prayed. Dear God... Oh, *Dick*....

CHAPTER 4
DEATH COMES LATE

EVEN NITA'S most despairing thoughts could scarcely have pictured a more hopeless position than that in which Richard Wentworth found himself. It was true that the criminals could not attack without exposing themselves to his answering fire. But they had no need to attack!

Standing rigidly in the middle of his hermetically sealed cell of brick and steel and bullet-proof glass, Wentworth let his eyes make a slow quest of walls and ceiling. He was aware of the grinning, brutal face of the man left to guard him—Mugsy was his name, wasn't it?—as he moved carelessly to the Wreck's chair and settled his heels on the desk. The guard was not precisely alert, but his very nonchalance in the face of an imprisoned Spider, spoke clearly of the utter hopelessness of his position!

But, damn it, he couldn't remain in this cell! Quite aside from the fact that suffocation threatened before the expiration of many hours, there was the attack upon the bus to be thwarted. All those poor victims of the Wreck's viciousness were fore-doomed if he did not escape!

Wentworth's quick mind already had canvassed the full possibilities of the situation. He could feign being overcome by suffocation, but it would be several hours before he was in serious danger that way. Mugsy would know that If he waited until then, it would be too late to help the bus passengers. Well, there was another chance he could take, once he was sure the Wreck and his henchmen had left the garage. Wentworth weighed his automatics in his fists and waited.

There was one fact that Wentworth knew about bullet-proof glass. It would resist the close-range shock of lead, but it would not, for instance, stand up under a continuous machine-gun fire. If he fired a series of .45 caliber bullets at the same spot, he would presently have a loophole through which he could shoot! At the same time, he would be protected from return attack so that if they wanted to get at him, they would have to open up his cage....

Wentworth's lips moved in a grim smile as he waited through the slow ticking of the seconds to make sure that the Wreck had departed. There was one defect in his plan. In this tightly enclosed space, the concussion of his guns would be tremendous, and the air would soon become almost unbreathable with the fumes of cordite. It was even conceivable that the six extra clips of bullets he carried might not be sufficient to break through the glass....

Deliberately, Wentworth turned his back on Mugsy and tucked the clips into his belt where they could be reached swiftly. Once he started to fire, he must work at top speed. He shredded his handkerchief and made plugs for his ears, held them also ready in his hand. There was a tight frown on Mugsy's face that made it strangely ape-like. Mugsy was trying to think and he wasn't used to it. He would have even more to think about presently.

Wentworth selected his target carefully, so as to make a loophole which would afford him a clear shot at the door. He was pretty sure that the Wreck had left by now, and taken with him all the men who were not on guard in the garage. Abruptly, Wentworth stuffed the plugs into his ears, caught a deep breath and swiveled up both automatics. Even for such precise work, there was no need for him to take deliberate aim.

He fired from the hip and the twin heavy guns leaped and jerked in his hands. Concussion battered him like gusts of a mighty storm. Blood hammered in his temples, in his throat. His vision wavered and blurred... and the guns clicked empty in his fists. With swift skill, he thumbed out the empty clips and stuffed in fresh ones, cocked each automatic with a swift blow of the heel of his hand... and was firing again.

With eyes squinted against the acid bite of exploded cordite, body leaning against the shock of guns and concussion, he peered toward his target. The glass had turned opaque, frosted over by shattering impact. A few shards had fallen, glittering, to the floor. But that was only the nearest layer of the laminated glass. A feeling of hopelessness fumbled through Wentworth's shock-dulled mind, but he did not falter in his work, his hands did not waver from the sure fulfillment of the thing he had begun.

Another swift drum roll poured twelve more bullets into an area two inches across. The man Mugsy was on his feet, brandishing a revolver he could not use. His mouth was open, but no sound reached Wentworth's deafened eardrums. The Spider's fingers fumbled a little with this second reloading. His chest was panting heavily and sweat made beads upon his forehead and beneath his eyes. His legs were braced far apart, but even so he swayed as he stood there.

Whatever else he was accomplishing, he was swiftly exhausting the oxygen of this narrow cell. His body was racked by strangling coughs from the fumes his guns released. But he was ready now. Mugsy was lunging across the outer room toward the door, but the guns were ready....

Wentworth had to fire more deliberate to make sure of his target. He... Why, he was on his knees! The two heavy automatics jolted alternately against his stiffened wrists.

Dimly, he saw Mugsy leap erratically into the air and slam against the door facing. He could not see him clearly for many reasons, but chiefly because that frosted spot of glass, where his bullets hit, was centered squarely on Mugsy's back and head as he leaned and clawed at the door jamb. The man's face twisted about and he lifted his gun. With the dull steadiness of an automaton, Wentworth continued to fire.

Mugsy's gun hand flew high and the revolver spun from his fingers. His body jerked spasmodically against the door jamb, quivering in echo to every shot. Wentworth was jerking with those concussion impacts now himself. It was only when Mugsy slumped down with his hands still clawing the wood, when he pitched sidewise to the floor and rolled that Wentworth realized what had happened. Mugsy's face was gone and his chest was a red mess. He... Why, by the heavens, Wentworth's bullets had drilled him through and through. Then... then the loophole was finished!

WENTWORTH TRIED twice before he could get his

weight-deadened body to his feet. There was a fury inside his head and… blood was coming from his nostrils and ears! Concussion, of course. He reeled as he clawed his way through the thick air toward that loophole. Each shallow breath threw him into paroxysms of coughing. There was something he should do at once, he knew, but somehow… Oh, yes, reload the guns! One of them had fallen from his hand. He let it lie and braced one hand against the glass screen.

He could barely focus his eyes on the hole his bullets had made. A half dozen of them had punched through in an area no more than an inch across. Even in his dazed numbness, Wentworth could smile a little, grimly, at that. Thanks to long practice, his reflexes took care of his aim, even when his mind had deserted its task. He pressed his mouth and nostrils close against the opening and gratefully sucked in fresh air. His senses reeled but somehow he managed to keep his face close to that loophole.

If enemies had come then, there would have been an end of the Spider! None came and after an eternity Wentworth's brain began to clear. It was necessary still to keep his nostrils close to that hole, but the shock of concussion was fading from his body, leaving it weary, yet alert… and he realized he was no nearer escape than before.

Either there was no one else in the building, or else the sound of the shots, muffled in this cell, had failed to reach their ears. Mugsy was dead, and from within Wentworth stood no chance at all of operating the mechanism that had imprisoned him. He had a shrewd idea that the key was somewhere about the Wreck's desk, probably in the drawer where the leader's hand had rested. For him, it might as well be on the opposite side of the world!

Perhaps, he might even be compelled to wait here until the Wreck returned from the slaughter! The lipless gash that was the Spider's mouth gaped in a grin of menace. The Spider still had twelve cartridges for his automatics and a loophole that commanded the office. He thought that the Wreck would find a welcome he would not relish! But he could not wait. It might already be too late to save those poor prisoners of the bus… Wentworth shook his head violently to clear it of the last fogginess. There had to be a way out of here.

Once more, studiously, Wentworth surveyed the section of the room in which he was imprisoned. The only article in it was an ice-water cooler which contained a ten gallon bottle of water. He stared at it and, abruptly, laughed. He stripped off cloak and coat, began to rip his shirt to shreds, then stuff the strips, one by one, through the loophole in the glass. Slowly a pile of cloth accumulated outside, and he left a last streamer dangling. The contents of his cigarette lighter trickled down to soak the pile of linen, then supplied the flame that touched it off.

Wentworth retreated from the glass, watched the flame run down his fuse and ignite the pile. The exhausted air was stultifying and, for the present, the loophole offered no relief. He waited while the flames crawled up the face of the bullet-proof screen, waited beside the bottle of water. It would take a while for that thick glass, with its interposed layers of mica, to heat through. When it did, a douse of ice-cold water would crack it. A slim steel blade on his pocket knife would sever the mica….

Maddening to wait here with the knowledge that every moment brought the bus passengers nearer their doom… His lungs labored, but at last he deemed the moment ripe and seized the heavy bottle of water from its stand. A deluge of it against the glass… With a brittle, snapping sound, a crack ran its jagged way up the bullet-proof screen!

Furiously, Wentworth flung himself at the task of severing the mica. Even when he had finished this, he must start another fire, and this time it must be inside the cell! With two severances a few feet apart, he thought that he would be able to wedge the panel open and so escape. If not, then he must devise some way of cracking the glass horizontally….

WENTWORTH LOST track of time as he labored, but at last he was ready to build the second fire. He crouched at he loophole, sucking in air, cleansing his lungs. It was madness to build the fire inside the cell, but he had no choice. He could not work through the loophole a second time and still get space enough between the two cracks to permit his ultimate escape. Smoke poisoning, and death, Wentworth recognized grimly, were definite possibilities!

The thought did not delay him at all. He shredded his coat for fuel and laid it against the glass at the point he had chosen; touched it off. He soaked his handkerchief in water and bound it over his face, lay down upon the floor. There the carbon dioxide was densest… but the smoke already thickening in the room was least.

Within a few seconds, Wentworth was gasping for breath. The fire was rapidly exhausting the last of the oxygen in the cell and it could not come in rapidly enough through the loop-hole. The fire was thick with smoke and there was little flame. Heaven only knew whether it would be hot enough to accomplish anything! Wentworth felt his senses reeling with the laboring of his lungs. But he had to hold to consciousness long enough to drench the heated face of the glass with the cold water. He *had to!*

There was fire in the lining of his throat and his lungs felt raw. He coughed almost without let-up. His sides were sore with it; his leanly powerful body weakened. When finally he raised himself to carry the bottle to the fire, he could clamber only to his knees. A paroxysm of coughing shook him terribly, and cold fear raced through him. Had he waited too long? Was his strength too far gone? Bent almost double by the violence of his strangling, Wentworth groped for the bottle, felt it slip from his hands. It did not break, but it gurgled and slopped from the mouth with a sound like mocking laughter.

Wentworth made no attempt to right the bottle. There wasn't time. He used his hat as a bucket and, with it, dashed water across the face of the glass. The sound of the cracking was less emphatic this time and the jagged line that meant freedom, or death, to Richard Wentworth, ran no higher than two feet above the floor. Wentworth stared at it with bleary eyes, dragged himself to the loophole. It might serve. It would have to serve....

WENTWORTH LOST all track of time. There was weakness and agony inside him and, time after time, he had to force his dragging body back to the loophole for breathing. How he finished the job of severing the mica sheets, how he rigged cloth across the face of the glass to make the horizontal crack, he probably never would recall. Somehow it was managed and there was a little more air now... more for the fire.

He remembered using the iron base of the water cooler as a sledge, hurling his failing body in a final surge against that stubborn shield. Finally, the doorway of glass yielded and he sprawled on the floor, broken, terribly weakened, but free... *Free!*

A wild urgency drove Wentworth on... that bus. He struggled to his feet and reached for the telephone on the Wreck's desk. His blurred eyes could scarcely find the dial and, when police headquarters answered, a violent racking cough almost strangled out his words. Finally, he made himself understood, got through to the office of Commissioner Kirkpatrick.

"Wentworth speaking," he gasped. "An attack is planned... buses in the Bronx." He shook with coughing that seemed to tear the lining of his throat. "Don't know line."

"Are you ill, Dick?" Kirkpatrick asked anxiously. "The buses? Too late! We found two Down Easters abandoned on the Post Road. Six people dead on them, shot, and no trace of any of the others. If you can throw any light on who did it...."

"Just a tip," Wentworth dragged out. "See you later. Sorry... so late."

He hung up and, for a while, clung to the desk for support. He had to have medical treatment, but first he would make sure that when the Wreck returned to these headquarters there was a fitting welcome awaiting him! Six dead; and the rest captives, destined to be changed into crippled monsters at the hands of the Wreck! The police would do everything possible to track them down at once. He might be able to help a little… when he could talk.

It was an incredible strain to put through the call to his own home and to grasp the message of his aged butler, Jenkyns… that Nita was not there but had called out Ram Singh and Jackson, who were waiting as ordered at Twenty-fourth and First Avenue. They had called back for instructions on failing to make connections. And none had come.

Sitting there in the sanctum of the Wreck, Wentworth forced himself to a realization of what Jenkyns' message meant. But it was fairly obvious, wasn't it? Nita had followed him here and called for help; but had disappeared before Ram Singh and Jackson arrived. Either she had followed the Wreck when he left, or she had been captured. One thing was certain. If she had not again communicated, it meant that she was now a prisoner of the Wreck, or else… or else was dead!

Wentworth drove himself to a search of the desk but it yielded nothing at all save a rent receipt which told him only that the owner of the garage was a company controlled by a certain politician named Morton Vantine. Vantine had been under fire recently as a protector of criminals….

Wentworth shook his head heavily. It might be a lead, but on the surface it meant nothing. His greatest hope must lie in the Wreck's speedy return into the trap that the Spider would set. WITH CLUMSY hands, Wentworth drew the cape about his naked, soot-streaked shoulders, dragged the wet black hat down about his temples. The automatics were thrust into his waistband… For an instant, he paused beside the corpse of

Mugsy, bent to imprint the Spider's seal upon his forehead, and his lips twisted bitterly over the action. Surely, it was an empty threat he made here since his best efforts had not availed to block the attack upon the bus, nor to save Nita!

When he pushed out of the garage, empty save for himself and the corpse of the gunman, Wentworth saw that angry streamers of red laced the sky with the threat of day. He bent his head and pushed heavy feet toward the spot where Ram Singh and Jackson would be waiting, and he staggered, shaken by the violence of his tearing cough.

At sight of him, both his men sprang from the car to his assistance. Until the moment when his eyes fell on the faithful, worried face of Jackson and saw the fiercely bearded Sikh, Wentworth had not realized the extent of his exhaustion. But he insisted on making his own way home alone in the car they had brought, leaving the Spider's coupé behind for their use.

As rapidly as he could, despite the torture of his scorched throat, he outlined the case, sent them to keep watch inside the garage.

"I want the Wreck himself, if possible," Wentworth finished raspingly. "If not him, then prisoners… prisoners who will *talk!*"

Ram Singh's brown powerful hand touched the hilt of the knife thrust into his sash. *"Han, sahib,"* he rumbled. "They shall talk!"

Wentworth drove fumblingly back to fortress-mansion behind Sutton Place that was his home, stripping off his disguise with feeble hands as he pushed through the dawn-empty streets. A spray of oil soothed his throat and, as soon as his voice was reasonably under control, he put in another call for Commissioner Kirkpatrick. His speech was hoarse, almost unrecognizable, but he forced himself to go on. Rapidly, while his aged butler, Jenkyns, hovered about solicitously, he reported Nita's disappearance and detailed all the things he had learned about the Wreck, and those things which he suspected.

The facilities of the police would accomplish far more in tracing Nita than he alone could do… One thing only did he hold back—his battle in the garage or any mention of the place. Jackson and Ram Singh would keep adequate watch there. They might ensnare the Wreck himself, but regardless of that, any prisoners they took would talk.

"I suggest a round-up of every crippled beggar on the streets," Wentworth concluded his message to Kirkpatrick. "From what you say, there must have been enough holdups by cripples to justify that. Some of them are sure to be the men of the Wreck and it's possible one can be persuaded to talk. I think you'll find that the Missing Persons Bureau has a heavy increase of cases, and it might be wise to check up on doctors or surgeons on that list… Yes, Kirk, I'll be down soon. I was gassed when I tried to follow one of the cripples."

He hung up then and Jenkyns pressed a delectable breakfast upon him. His ruddy face was puckered with worry. "You must eat, Master Richie," he insisted, "and you must rest! You can't keep on like this. No sleep, no food. It will be the death of you."

Wentworth smiled faintly while he forced himself to eat despite the torture of each swallow. Pheasant eggs whipped in sherry; breasts of squab prepared as only Jenkyns could. The coffee was fragrant and double-strength.

He needed rest, but lack of it would never cause his death. There were too many other, more vigorous enemies! How could he think of rest when Nita was in the hands of that monster? God alone knew where she was at this moment, Nita in the power or that maker of cripples… His brain was sodden with fatigue and a deepening drowsiness stole over him.

"Jenkyns, you wretch," he mumbled, "you've given me an opiate!"

Jenkyns contrived a worried smile.

"Master Richie, you must rest!"

WENTWORTH'S POWERFUL will might have fought off the drug long enough to take an antidote, but he realized the truth of what Jenkyns said. In his present condition he would fall too easy prey to the enemy. Better to lose a few hours… It was early afternoon when Wentworth awoke, richly refreshed, and after a rub-down and cold shower, he was ready once more for the battle. There had been no messages from Ram Singh or Jackson; none from Nita. Only Kirkpatrick had called to say that he would be in his office during the afternoon. No new leads; nothing….

The balmy warmth of the summer day was a mockery to Wentworth as he took a taxi to reclaim his Hispano-Suiza roadster from the garage where he had left it the night before. Already, his mind was plunged deep into the problem ahead, and there was a numb agony in his heart at the thought of Nita that he dared not allow to rise, lest it drive him mad. There was still a soreness in his throat that made his voice uncertain and, sometimes, rasping, and his chest felt weak. Otherwise he was all right… yet the Wreck had taken heavy toll of the Spider in those few hours!

He left the cab a block from the alley garage and went briskly on foot to the place. There was no difficulty only, when he tooled the sleek roadster out into the sunlight, he saw Nita's handkerchief on the seat and caught a hint of her perfume… and that was a fresh torture.

His lips were grim as he hurled the Hispano lithely through traffic toward police headquarters. It was strange that he had not heard from Ram Singh or Jackson, but if they had made a capture, they would have reported. It was possible that the Wreck had discovered the trap and avoided it….

It was when he was rolling down Fourth Avenue, near Twenty-third, that he heard the blasting of gun-shots, sudden and ominous in the drowsy heat of early afternoon. In an instant, he had spotted the source of the disturbance and whirled into the cross street. Instantly, he was in the middle of a battle.

A car hurtled straight toward him, and gun-flame spurted from its windows. He saw a taxi driver ahead of him crumple; a pedestrian took a bullet in the face. Standing in a truck, a neatly dressed man with a rifle cuddled against his cheek, was firing calmly into the ranks of the forming pursuit. A policeman checked in mid stride, stumbled and pitched headlong. Even as Wentworth whipped out his automatic, he saw the rifleman swing to clear the way for the escaping car, saw the sights center unerringly on his own chest!

CHAPTER 5
SLAVES OF FEAR

IN THE instant while his automatic swiveled toward the rifleman, Wentworth knew a breath of thankfulness that he was not driving his Lancia with its bullet-proof glass. The glass could not resist rifle fire, but it would have kept him from shooting in the only way he could that would be in time—through his own windshield!

It seemed to him that, almost before he had squeezed the trigger, the glass starred and split before him. His body jarred to the confined concussion. The rifleman pivoted sideways from his gun rest on the side of the truck. Wentworth was strangely conscious of the whiteness of the man's hands as he gripped the wooden barrier, then the head sagged from view and, presently the hands loosened and vanished, too. The rifle performed a slow somersault to the pavement.

The crack of a high-speed bullet whipped Wentworth about toward a fresh target. He saw no new rifleman, but he knew that snapping lead could have come from no other source. He wrenched the wheel of the Hispano to disconcert farther aim and fired across his chest at the driver of the escaping bandit car. He saw the man flung brutally backward under the impact and the machine swerved wildly, was instantly righted again as a second bandit, under cover of his already dead driver, leaned forward to seize the wheel.

Another high-speed bullet cracked and the rim of the Hispano's steering wheel split under his hand. He flung another shot at the speeding car, swung sharply to the right and then whipped over his crumbling wheel for a U-turn. Previously, he had been too deep in battle to take in the scene of the street, but when he did, shock sent a curse hoarsely to his lips.

The street was a shambles. Before the bank, two men in uniform and three civilians lay motionless upon the pavement. The taxi, with its dead driver, had hurtled the curb to drive a screaming woman through a plate-glass window. Crouched near it, a cripple on crutches was firing indiscriminately into the crowd upon the sidewalk. It was wanton, mad slaughter and the cripple's participation betrayed its author. Here was more work of that monster called the Wreck!

Savagely, Wentworth threw two shots toward the cripple, saw him hammered from the support of his crutch and flung writhing upon the pavement. The Hispano had almost completed the sweep of the U-turn. The tires whined shrilly to the drive of the powerful engine. He peered narrowly toward the fugitive car, saw it yawing wildly as it drove at furious speed toward Fourth Avenue.

He glimpsed the traffic officer, already prostrate under a storm of lead… then a blast shook the Hispano! The remnants of the windshield hurled blunt-edged shards about him as it crashed inward. The dash-board glass smashed to bits and the air about him was alive with bullets. He felt a tire go with a hissing explosion. Violently, it swerved from the tight circle in which Wentworth held it. Before he could regain control it had smashed head-on into a small parked car!

The steering wheel completed its disintegration, as momen-

NITA VAN SLOAN —

tum hurled Wentworth bodily upon it. Stunned, reeling from the crash, Wentworth wrenched himself free and spilled out upon the pavement. He flung prone, but the gunfire had shifted to another target. He was out of the chase, no longer interesting....

In an instant, he had spotted two of the riflemen at adjoining windows across the street. His automatic kicked against his palm and the two men were punched backward out of sight. He twisted again toward the bandit car, but it had vanished. As he staggered to his feet, a radio prowl car roared past, its siren shrieking in pursuit.

When it had gone, there was a sickening quiet in the street. There was hoarse cries and women's screams but after the roaring catastrophe of the guns it seemed insignificant, puny. Wentworth's swift accustomed fingers were reloading the automatic while his eyes combed the street. But through the panic milling of the crowds he caught no further hint of hostility. Stiff-legged, gun ready in his fist, he moved toward the stalled truck from which the rifleman had done his deadly execution. There was a chance that man still lived… concerning the others there could be no question. His targets had been too fleeting and small to risk winging shots.

WENTWORTH WAS shaken by the horror of the scene he had witnessed. Such wanton slaughter as this was no part of the usual bank robbers' plan, yet there could be no doubt that these wild killings had been deliberately ordered: the cripple on the sidewalk spreading massacre in the crowd; the riflemen… Wentworth's lips were grim with fury as he sprang suddenly into the rear of the truck with his gun ready.

The rifleman lay half on his side, half on his back and his eyes held the glaze of approaching death. His breath rattled in his throat. His left trouser leg was empty from an amputation,

69

pinned up neatly, and the man's whole appearance presented an enigma. From conservative, neatly shined shoe to the dark fedora crushed beneath his head, he presented the picture of a moderately successful businessman. Either it was clever disguise, or... Wentworth bent over him.

"You're dying," he said, and his voice turned harsh. "Dying as you deserve. But you still can suffer... You'll talk or you'll suffer. Who is the Wreck? Where is he?"

The man's eyes opened sluggishly, but the glaze did not leave them. The smile, that stirred his lips was gentle. "Martha," he whispered. "Martha, now you can... can...."

"Where is the Wreck?"

The man thrust up on a stiff arm, stared wildly about him. "The Wreck," he gasped. "The..." A bloody cough broke his breath. He writhed, struggled for a hard moment, and was still.

Wentworth straightened slowly, and the frown between his brows was puzzled. This man was a wanton murderer and yet he could die with a woman's name and a soft smile on his lips... The enigma remained with him throughout the police investigation on the spot and afterward, when he accompanied Commissioner Kirkpatrick back to his office.

"It's important to have that man identified," Wentworth insisted. "I don't think they'll find his fingerprints in criminal files, but it would be a good idea to check bonding companies and the civilian identification files at Washington."

Kirkpatrick frowned at him bleakly from behind the heavy desk in his gaunt square of an office. "I'll confess I don't get the point, Dick," he said, in his usual crisp accents, "but it certainly shall be done."

He leaned forward to speak into his annunciator and Wentworth allowed a brief smile to cross his firm lips. Kirkpatrick was preeminently a man of action, an organizer. It showed in every line of his saturnine face. He was also the best police commissioner that New York had ever known.

"Your hunches," Kirkpatrick admitted, knuckling the spikes of his neat black mustache, "have a way of panning out, Dick. You mentioned the Missing Persons Bureau. There has been a two-hundred-percent increase in cases, and there are seven surgeons on the list."

"Two hundred percent!" Wentworth murmured. "I think I can shorten that list for you materially. Have your Missing Persons Bureau check the descriptions of those missing three weeks or more against those of the cripples your men have been arresting… and disregard the artificial crippling."

Kirkpatrick was leaning forward sharply, his frosty blue gaze on Wentworth's. "What are you implying, Dick," he demanded shortly. "That these cripples are fakes? They aren't. We haven't found a single one."

Wentworth shook his head quietly. "No, Kirk. They're real enough. But they weren't crippled by accidents or disease. They were deliberately crippled by this criminal who calls himself a Wreck! And I think these seven missing surgeons, or some of them, did the work!"

Kirkpatrick said gruffly, "That doesn't make sense, Dick. Why in God's name should a man do a thing like that? What profit could he find in crippling people?" He dragged a palm hard across his bony forehead. "We haven't been able to get any of the cripples to admit they even know a man named the Wreck. A good many of them are drug addicts... God, Dick, we've got to do something and do it quickly! If these disappearances and crimes keep up, the entire reputation of the city will be ruined! The World's Fair crowd is on my neck. They say it spoils business. But these cripples, Dick! If people really are being kidnapped and maimed...."

His eyes flicked suddenly to Wentworth's and there was pain there. "Dick," he whispered. "Dick, not Nita...."

Wentworth said hoarsely, "For God's sake, Kirk, don't you think I know?"

He strode across the room and stood staring out of the broad window down toward the street. His lean hands were knotted whitely behind him. When he spoke, his voice came out calmly despite its hoarseness.

"If the cripples won't talk," he said, "it's because they're enslaved. I don't know whether the agency is fear or drugs; perhaps both. It will be easy enough to verify my guess about surgery. Have a few of the cripples X-rayed. That won't show the agency or the crippling, but it will prove whether they can be readily cured by surgery. If it's possible, at all, it will be a strong argument for my theory. Perhaps..." He wheeled, his face alert. "If we can cure some of them, maybe the promise of help will make them talk! Have some X-rayed, then sent here to you for questioning. It's a chance, Kirk!"

"It's a chance," Kirkpatrick agreed and once more bent to his annunciator. "No, no, I can't see anyone! Who? Morton Vantine? I don't give a damn who he is, and attend to that order at once. WENTWORTH CAUGHT the name and came slowly toward Kirkpatrick's desk. Vantine was the politician whose corporation owned the Wreck's garage. He didn't necessarily know anything about the tenants, but there was a chance… that Vantine himself was involved! But Wentworth had not mentioned the garage incident to Kirkpatrick. Ram Singh and Jackson were on watch there. A breath of coldness touched Wentworth's spine.

"Hasn't Vantine something to do with the city hospitals?" he asked softly.

"He's got his finger in every graft pie around the city," Kirkpatrick grunted. "Why?"

"We're going to need the hospitals." Wentworth said quietly. "I'm going to propose, Kirk, that every cripple we pick up who can be cured shall be given immediate hospitalization. The facilities are inadequate, of course. But it would give us some grip over the Wreck. If his cripples can be cured, I'll donate a million dollars toward the work."

Wentworth's face was white, and Kirkpatrick smiled sardonically. "That's a big sum of money, even for you, Dick," he said. "And it's just to get a grip on the Wreck, is it?"

Wentworth flushed slightly. "All right," he acknowledged gruffly. "But I've seen those victims of this monster. Have you?"

Kirkpatrick kept his eyes on Wentworth as he ordered Vantine admitted. He stood and put his hand on Wentworth's shoulder. "Dick," he said quietly. "I have never known another man like you. Is there no end to what you will do for humanity?"

Wentworth moved impatiently under the touch of Kirkpatrick's hand, but he knew the unspoken meaning behind Kirkpatrick's words. The commissioner had long been convinced that Richard Wentworth was the Spider. There had been occasions when the proof was almost in his hands, and it had not been from any laxness in duty that he had failed. Kirkpatrick would not know how to betray his oath of office. And that threat hung ever over Wentworth's head, for he knew that if Kirkpatrick ever gathered the evidence to convict him, the Spider's days were finished.

Meantime, they were staunch friends, there was this armed truce between them, and they would do what they could, side by side, to counteract crime.

Wentworth laughed shortly. "You forget, Kirk, I can deduct it from my income tax."

The door was opened and an orderly said, "Mr. Vantine, sir."

Vantine lunged through the doorway with a choppy, pounding stride that was almost a run. He was a bull-like man with heavy jaws and, contrary to appearance, all his gestures were sharp and quick, like the shallow stab of his dark eyes. His scanty hair was a neutral gray and his voice had a perpetual hoarseness.

"Damn it, Kirkpatrick," he bellowed. "No wonder this confounded department never catches a crook! A taxpayer with information, and you keep him waiting. Keep me waiting! By God, I won't stand for it!"

Kirkpatrick regarded him steadily with a slight chill smile on his lips. "This isn't the third district club room, Vantine," he said shortly. "Be civil or get out."

Vantine checked just before the desk, his short arms swinging, half-flexed, at his sides. "All right; so you're a wise lad," he bellowed hoarsely. "That's why you never catch the Spider. He goes on killing...."

"You've seen him?" Kirkpatrick cut in shortly.

Vantine rolled his shoulders as if his coat fit too tightly. "I found a man he killed," he said shortly, "with that nasty sneering red Seal on his forehead! I was making an inspection of some real estate properties and found this garage without a soul in it. When I went to the office. I found the attendant murdered... by the Spider! This is a hell of a city, when a decent law-abiding man...."

"Do you mean yourself, Vantine, or the dead man?" Kirkpatrick was entirely calm, knuckling his mustache. "I seem to recall that a grand jury is working on some graft charges against you."

"A frame-up," Vantine shouted. "Listen, I didn't come here to bandy words with you! I came to report a murder."

"And I appreciate your diligence," Kirkpatrick assured him quietly. "Did you also notify the precinct? Yes, I'm glad you did. As for the Spider... It's strange if he killed a law-abiding man. He is usually more careful. Tell me about this garage."

Wentworth's hands twisted into a slow white knot behind him. No need to ask what garage Vantine meant, of course, but in heaven's name, what had become of Jackson and Ram Singh! Vantine said he had found the place empty... *said*.

Wentworth narrowed his eyes speculatively and tried to drape the robes of the Wreck on the heavy-built body of Morton Vantine. He frowned. It was possible, in fact easy, to rig an artificial hump on a man's shoulders and hence give him the appearance of being a much taller man, stooped by deformity, Given that appliance, and a knack for imitation.

Wentworth's eyes dropped to Vantine's hands. The fingers did not accord at all with his general build. True they had a certain fat padding, but they were long and tapered.

Kirkpatrick and Vantine were glaring at each other while Vantine threw out the facts of his discovery, the trap of bullet-proof glass....

"A law-abiding man has few uses for such contrivances," Kirkpatrick suggested mildly.

Vantine sneered. "Maybe, that was why the Spider shot him through the back. Four or five times. His face was a mess."

But Jackson and Ram Singh... Wentworth felt pallor draining his face. Twenty-four hours he had been locked in battle with the Wreck and one by one his comrades-at-arms vanished, Nita first....

"If I may interrupt," he said. "Who is the tenant of the garage?

Vantine swung toward him. "It was my tenant that was killed," he said violently.

Wentworth nodded. Yes, it would be like that, of course. "Kirk," he said. "If the Spider was there it must be because the Wreck had been there also. Fingerprints are possible... By the way, Mr. Vantine, it might be well if your own prints were taken so that the police will not be led astray by their presence in the office."

Vantine snorted. "To hell with you! Nobody is going to take my fingerprints and frame me. Kirkpatrick, you've got my report. If you want to find me, you can. I've done my duty. See if you can do as well!" He swung toward the door, making a lot of noise with his heels.

WENTWORTH SHOOK his head slowly. "I would suspect Vantine a lot more if he had consented to have his fingerprints taken. The Wreck has undoubtedly been in that office, and by having his prints taken, Vantine would protect himself against any supposed confusion with the Wreck. However, the Wreck has probably taken care of that already by coating his fingerprints. As it is, I don't know. He has a suspicious record." Wentworth dropped into a chair and slumped forward, elbows on his knees. Jackson and Ram Singh and Nita… and he had learned nothing; *nothing*.

Kirkpatrick said slowly, "Dick, I hate to say this, but that trap in the garage was an air-tight affair and there were definite traces of fire on the floor. When you telephoned me, you had been… *gassed*. Do you still advise a fingerprint check-up?"

Wentworth did not lift his head, "By all means, Kirk," he said wearily.

Kirkpatrick came around the desk to rest a hand lightly on Wentworth's shoulder. "Sooner or later, Dick, you're going to slip up," he said. "All criminals do ultimately. When you do, Dick…."

Wentworth moved his shoulders impatiently. "I wish you could get over your obsession, Kirk, that I am the Spider. The man is good, but he's not as good as I am. Surely, you give me credit for more brains? Do I go around killing people because I can't prove cases in court?"

Kirkpatrick smiled wryly. "Not that I've ever been able to prove, Dick," he admitted. "As for the courts... I find them pretty feeble myself sometimes."

Wentworth's mocking brows quirked, "You, Kirk? Surely not. You the right arm of the law! Maybe it's left also."

Kirkpatrick's face was sternly somber. "Don't play the fool, Dick. I know the Spider's methods are more efficient. While I grope for evidence, and thousands more suffer from the inroads of these master criminals, the Spider can strike. But, Dick, men can be mistaken! Even the courts can convict the innocent. Suppose, some day, the Spider strikes... *the wrong man!*"

Wentworth said, steadily, "Let the Spider worry about that, Kirk. I believe he is a man of conscience." But Kirkpatrick's words had struck home. He had voiced the one doubt that harassed the Spider through the months and years of his crusades. So far he had always been right... He thrust the thought into the back of his mind; he could never exclude it.

"Can't we get a report on that rifleman I stopped?" he asked curtly. "And what about these X-rays? They've had time enough... Kirk, if we prove that these cripples can be cured, the money I contribute won't be nearly enough. And I won't have time to administer it, to keep out the grafters that always crop up. We'll have to find someone who'll undertake the task of raising more money and seeing that it accomplishes the mission for which it is intended."

Kirkpatrick nodded and the signal of his annunciator whirred.

Kirkpatrick depressed the cam, and a man's voice issued. "Identification bureau. Powell speaking. We identified that rifleman from civil records at Washington. Thaddeus Goodsale of Mohawk, Ohio. Vice-president of a bank there. Left home to visit the Fair a month ago with daughter, Martha. Reported missing. Leg amputated since then."

As the man spoke, Wentworth drew slowly to his feet. The whole picture was falling into place now. There was no question of identification being correct, for the dying man had whispered the name of his daughter, Martha. But the thing that shook Wentworth with fury was the recognition of the Wreck's system. Here was the key to the unfaltering obedience of the cripples he enslaved!

"Do you see it, Kirk?" he asked hoarsely. "The Wreck held Martha Goodsale hostage for her father's good behavior! If he faltered in the job given him, his daughter would be, not killed, but turned into a cripple! No wonder the cripples obey! I'm sure the lists of missing will show dozens of cases with members of the *same families* missing. That's why the Wreck is operating in the time of the World's Fair. People come in parties, with their families or loved ones. They won't be missed for a considerable while if the Wreck seizes them all. By the time the Wreck is through with them, they have no choice except abject slavery! As cripples, their own jobs back home will be closed to them. Their loved ones are hostage, with the same horrible threat over their heads!"

"Good God, Dick," Kirkpatrick whispered, "you've got it!

Without a doubt, you've got it! This Wreck is a fiend out of hell, and…."

The whir of the annunciator interrupted him and a man's voice came from it crisply. "Hospital calling. X-ray reports."

Kirkpatrick snatched up the phone and listened while blood crept angrily up to his temples and the muscles knotted along his jaw.

"Very well," he clipped. "Continue to X-ray all cripples. I'll see that money is supplied. Send those three men to me."

He set the phone back in its cradle precisely, but with restrained vehemence. "You're right on all counts, Dick. The surgeons found the first three cases they examined could be rectified easily though perhaps not perfectly. Their own phrase is that bones had been broken and—reset with criminal carelessness—so that twisted limbs resulted. I'm having the three brought here for questioning. You mentioned an administrator for this fund, Dick. I have a man in mind. A partial cripple himself and a philanthropist. In every case where he can, he employs cripples to do his work, has doctors do everything possible for them. Ernest Hathaway. A high official of the Jupiter auto company."

"He'd have organizing ability, too," Wentworth acknowledged. "A good idea, Kirk. We'd better call on him."

THE ARRIVAL of the three prisoners was announced and as the door opened, he now saw the cripples. Kirkpatrick was standing at the end of his desk and his hand, resting on its surface, went white with pressure.

The man who entered first, knelt with twisted and useless

legs on a wheel platform and dragged himself along with his hands. Immediately behind him, a man awkwardly used a pair of crutches. His legs bent outward just above the knee and there was no strength in them. The third man limped painfully, on a twisted foot and his left arm jutted out stiffly at a fantastic angle. The hand was a drawn knot.

A painful sight….

At Kirkpatrick's gesture, the three were lined up against the far side of the room and the guards went out. The cripples were sullen. The man on the rolling platform hung his head and leaned far forward on braced arms. Staring at him, Wentworth was troubled by a strange sense of recognition.

Kirkpatrick was talking, identifying the three men by the names they had given. The man Wentworth felt he knew was Smith, the one on crutches Jones, and the man with the twisted arm had listed himself as Brown. Wentworth frowned, recognizing that though each man had given an alias none of them had a criminal's facility for inventing aliases or names.

Kirkpatrick hooked a thigh over a corner of the desk. "You men have all been questioned," he said pleasantly, "about the Wreck to whom you owe allegiance. We know that he crippled you, and we know that probably he holds a hostage for each of you."

The man, Smith, jerked up his head and even on his low platform he gave an appearance of power and determination. His drawn face was hard-boned, stubborn, and Wentworth felt again the sense of recognition. He closed his eyes, trying to trace out the memory while Kirkpatrick's voice went quietly on.

"So you see," he said, "I know why you won't talk. What I'm going to point out to you is this. If you will tell us where to find the Wreck, we can save these hostages. What you probably don't know is that all of you can be made whole, strong men again. The X-rays proved it. Smith, your legs can be made straight and strong so you can walk again. Yours, too, Jones. Brown, your twisted foot can be made normal, and most of the strength restored to that arm."

It was Jones who stumbled forward on his crutches, his voice high and eager. "You can fix me so I'll walk again. You can?"

Smith's voice came out, sharp and commanding. "Shut up, Jones."

Wentworth opened his eyes with a smile. He had it now.

Kirkpatrick disregarded the interruption. "Of course, we can't do anything for you without your consent...."

"Oh, I'll consent!" Jones' dirt-smeared face was eager and his eyes had lost their hang-dog look.

"We won't even put a price on medical attention," Kirkpatrick went on. "By that, I mean that regardless of whether you talk or not, this will be done for you. I want you to realize that the yoke of the Wreck can be broken! Now, gentlemen, it's up to you. Will you tell me where to find the Wreck? How I can break him? Perhaps, one of you even knows his real identity?"

Wentworth said softly, "How about you, Sergeant Sullivan?"

The man, Smith, whirled his platform about with a rough sound of wheels on wood that was like a cry of strangled fear.

Kirkpatrick uttered a startled oath. "By the heavens, it is Sergeant Sullivan who resigned a few years ago to enter business! Sergeant," Kirkpatrick's voice crisped with command, "for these others there may be some excuse, but for you...."

Sullivan said curtly, "I dropped that title of sergeant three years ago, Mr. Kirkpatrick. You can skip that kind of talk. And you won't get anything out of any of us! We don't know anything about this Wreck, whoever he is. We were going about our business when we were arrested, and we're not vagrants. There are no charges against us. I demand that we be released!"

His tone was belligerent, but there was a pleading in his eyes as they rested on Kirkpatrick's face. It was plain that the respect and admiration in which all the force held Kirkpatrick was still felt by this man. It was equally plain that he would not talk. His hands, gripping the sides of his thick platform, were reddening with pressure.

Jones fumbled forward on his crutches. "I'll talk, sir," he cried. "Just get these others out, and I'll talk."

Kirkpatrick nodded and stepped toward his desk to signal the guards... and Sullivan skidded into action! A powerful thrust of his hands sent him forward. The edge of his platform knocked Jones' left crutch out from under him and dropped him heavily toward the floor. As he fell, Sullivan's right hand whipped to his platform again and, from beneath its edge, jerked out a long-bladed knife.

Wentworth hurled himself forward... too late. The knife was waiting for Jones as he fell and the point gashed through his throat. Wentworth struck, but Sullivan thrust himself violently backward and while his platform still rolled, he whipped back his arm for a throw—*at Kirkpatrick!*

"I'm sorry, sir," he gasped. "Sorry, but it's your life or hers, and...."

Kirkpatrick was frozen in surprise beside his desk, his body twisted as he pressed the button for the guards. He could not dodge... Sullivan's knife arm whipped forward!

CHAPTER 6
MURDER MANIA

SPRAWLING TOWARD the dying cripple he had tried to save, Richard Wentworth realized maddeningly that he would be too late to save Kirkpatrick from Sullivan's knife. Not that it would keep him from trying! Even as he fell toward the cripple, Wentworth threw out his left arm as a brace while his right flashed toward the automatic beneath his left armpit. The stiffened left arm rolled him, the gun leaped clear of its holster... but Sullivan's hand was already flashing forward for the throw!

The whole scene was etched indelibly in Wentworth's mind, Kirkpatrick crouched over the desk, balanced on one foot in an impossible position either for dodging or fighting; just beside him the gasping blood-drowned breathing of the knifed cripple was sickeningly loud. Sullivan's cart was almost against the far partition of the office, his knife flashing forward for the throw, and beside him was the cripple with the twisted foot and the withered arm—the man, Brown, who had neither moved nor spoken since his first entrance into the office.

It was Brown who acted when split seconds spelled the difference between Kirkpatrick's life and death. Brown pivoted on his good foot and that stiffly outthrust arm of his circled weirdly toward Sullivan. The timing was perfect. The arm caught the knife the instant before it was released, and the blade buried hilt deep in Brown's flesh! The impact of the blow spun him away across the room and through the heart of that breathless pause, Wentworth's gun spoke authoritatively.

It had been pointed for Sullivan's shoulder but the same force that had sent Brown reeling on his awkward twisted foot across the room, had wrenched Sullivan about on his wheeled pedestal. The bullet struck his shoulder but only gouged through its upper muscle. It tore on to take Sullivan solidly in the jawbone just forward of the ear at a range of less than ten feet.

Sullivan's bristling hair seemed to leap free of his head. His whole body lifted and lunged sideways, upsetting the cart to which his legs were strapped so that it lifted like a merciful curtain between Wentworth's eyes and the wreckage his bullet had wrought.

The concussion racketed through the office. Brown finally lost his footing and sprawled to his knees, pitched sideways to the floor and afterward there was silence in which the rattling last breath of the knifed cripple died. Then there was only the faint whirring of a wheel on Sullivan's platform that still spun lazily. Perhaps three seconds had elapsed since Jones had said, "I'll talk!"

Wentworth pushed stiffly to his feet as the door hammered open and police guards charged through with guns in their fists. Kirkpatrick's voice rang out authoritatively, but Wentworth had turned toward the man, Brown, who lay where he had fallen on the floor. His eyes were wide as he watched the red drip from the sleeve where the knife had transfixed his arm.

"I guess I did it," he whispered stupidly as Wentworth bent gently toward him. "I guess I did."

"You did," Wentworth assured him grimly. "Let me see that arm. Come now." There was a fierce hope in Wentworth's breath, but it was blasted long before the doctor had finished working on Brown's arm. Brown was willing enough to talk, but the plain truth was that he knew next to nothing. A drink he had purchased in a drugstore apparently had knocked him out on the way to his hotel and he had recovered consciousness in the power of the Wreck. There had been an operation and a recuperative period at some country sanitarium, but he could offer no help in finding it. The trip to New York City had been hours long and performed in a closed truck. Fortunately, he had been in New York alone....

A watch was set over the drugstore, but as Wentworth pointed out, it was entirely possible that someone sitting beside him had dropped a drug into Brown's drink. Or the soda dispenser might have been responsible. Men were delegated also to work at questioning such cripples as could be rehabilitated. There was a chance that one of them might talk; there seemed little hope that any would know more than Brown.

"HIS PLANS seem airtight," Wentworth told Kirkpatrick, as they sped to the office of Ernest Hathaway to seek his help in arranging for rehabilitation of the cripples. "The Wreck apparently lets none of the cripples know much. Those that might talk intelligibly, like Sullivan, are bound to him by hostages! You heard what Sullivan said. *'It's your life or hers'....* "

Kirkpatrick's lips were drawn thin, deepening the lines about their corners. "I seem to remember a daughter," he said bitterly. "You realize what this means, Dick? We have to be on a perpetual lookout for assassins. The Wreck can remove not only ourselves, but anyone else who stands in his way, simply by turning loose some of these hostage—fired madmen! He has built himself an almost invincible army of crime: men who will kill and die rather than talk; who will perform their tasks at imminent risk of their lives!"

Wentworth nodded grimly. "I think the Wreck may even promise the cripples that if they die in the line of duty, the hostages will go free. Whether he performs his promise, I don't know, but if he does, we should soon be able to pick up Sullivan's daughter."

"It's a thought," Kirkpatrick acknowledged. "She would have every reason to talk."

The offices outside the doors of Ernest Hathaway's sanctum were a curious place. There wasn't a bookkeeper or a stenographer who didn't show the traces of crippling or deformity. A girl in a wheelchair operated a typewriter on a special desk and, as Wentworth watched her, she whipped the chair about and shot it toward a filing-cabinet much more quickly than mere walking. A bookkeeper gripped a pen in an artificial hand, and the reception clerk picked up a crutch to usher them toward Hathaway's door.

Hathaway himself was seated behind a desk of rich mahogany

DR. BOURSE

TEMPLE

in an elegantly simple office. The floor covering was an Aubusson rug. He had a high, challenging carriage to his head and his smile was wide and frank. It was a powerful, intelligent face, and the shoulders were nicely proportioned, only there was a slight

HATHAWAY

MORTON VANTINE

stiffness to his rising, a faintest drag to his feet as he moved around the desk to greet them.

"Chairs, Temple," he gestured toward an assistant and the man deftly slid seats forward for Wentworth and Kirkpatrick.

Wentworth glanced at him curiously, but saw no evidence

that Temple had been a cripple unless a minor awkwardness in head movements was the after result of some deformity.

"Anything else, sir?" Temple asked, his voice low and Wentworth saw that his large dark eyes rested on Hathaway with something close to adoration.

Wentworth thought shrewdly that, though Hathaway might have staffed his office with cripples for philanthropic reasons, it undoubtedly paid him extra dividends in loyalty and conscientious work. As Kirkpatrick had pointed out, the man was ideal for their purposes and he agreed readily to the proposal.

"I'll have to obtain leave, but it will be worth it," Hathaway told them earnestly. "And I'll want to take Temple with me. I couldn't do a thing without him."

Temple flushed and Hathaway smiled up at him. "Wouldn't think this man had ever been bed-ridden, would you," he asked. "Infantile paralysis almost did him in. Fourteen months in an iron lung. There's a great deal that can be done with this money you're donating, Mr. Wentworth. I'll be glad to contribute also. I think we'll need to organize a drive for more money. And there will have to be added facilities... This criminal of yours—what do you call him, the Wreck—I can't actually believe in the existence of a man who would do the things of which you accuse him, but I'll welcome the chance to straighten out a few more crooked lives. Physically crooked, of course!"

He laughed, and there was excitement in the sound. "I'll try to get Doctor Bourse... Doctor Otto Bourse, that is... to donate his time. He's probably the world's greatest orthopedic surgeon. There have been accusations made against him in the past. Vivisection. May be true! But it was done to improve his technique, his help to human beings!

These fool societies....

It was apparent that Hathaway was riding a hobby that he would pursue endlessly, but Wentworth was satisfied that he would take hold of the rehabilitation of the cripples with equal energy. When they left, he said as much to Kirkpatrick. "By the way, Kirk," he added. "It might be just as well to know something about this Doctor Otto Bourse. I've heard his name, of course. Surgery has been performed on the cripples and, in a sense, it might come under the head of vivisection."

Kirkpatrick laughed, "Just groping, Dick? Think we'd better check on Hathaway, too? After all, he is surrounded by cripples!"

Wentworth stared soberly before him. "I think that would be an excellent idea," he said slowly. "After all, we can't look for the Wreck among the ranks of ordinary criminals. The man has a twist. I think I caught a glimpse of the Wreck once. He either is a cripple, or masquerades as one—a hunchback. I don't exclude anyone from suspicion!"

THEY RETURNED to the routine questioning of the cripples and though a few were willing to talk, none of them could contribute more than had Brown. A checkup was begun on all sanatoriums within a two-hundred-mile radius of New York City, but it was a task that would require months unless luck played with them. Police were set to work to question residents along the route of the Down East Bus Company since Wentworth was sure the kidnapping could not have been performed on the Post Road. That, too, was a task without end and meantime the questioning of the cripples went on.

Fresh floods of them poured into the city as rapidly as they could be arrested—and thousands of them had to be released upon the streets. There was no charge on which they could be held for long. And crime mounted with an awful momentum; robberies of all characters from mere sneak-thievery and burglary to armed hold-ups. And people disappeared by twos and threes; by families; by scores....

The newspapers screamed for relief and businessmen besieged the city government with protests. It had become such a menace that people walked fearfully upon the streets and, after dark, New York became a deserted city. The World's Fair crowds had dwindled until officials debated closing it—and Commissioner Kirkpatrick took the brunt of it. There could be no better man for the job than himself, yet there was every chance that he would be removed as a scapegoat. And cripples were lynched by terrified mobs.

Wentworth labored endlessly in his attempts to track down the Wreck… and there was no word from Nita, and none from Ram Singh or Jackson. Not even threats from the Wreck. Some small things Wentworth accomplished. Once he stumbled upon a kidnapping and took prisoner the crippled agents of the Wreck—and shots from the dark murdered them before he could begin their questioning.

The warehouse to which the buses had been driven was found, identified by the blood of the victims upon the floor, but it had long been abandoned. Wentworth spent days in trailing cripples about the streets and located a half-dozen dormitory lodging-houses in which they were quartered. But when police raided them, they found the men in charge of the dormitories were others like the small-town banker with the rifle whom Wentworth had killed. They would not, dared not talk. Prisons were filled with convicted cripples, and there were concentration camps.

All was frustration and terror and murder, and twenty-two days had passed since Nita had vanished and the first horror of the Wreck had thrown its black shadows over the city.

It was on the twenty-third day that, in his customary conference with Kirkpatrick, Wentworth determined upon a final desperate attempt.

"Yesterday," he said in the dead, level voice that had become his speech in these days of failure. "I located three more of the cripple dormitories. Their addresses are in the notes I gave you. Suppose this time you do not raid them? Suppose I make myself up as the Wreck and visit them?"

"You're mad," Kirkpatrick said curtly. "You glimpsed this Wreck once at a distance. Your disguise would not stand up under inspection for five minutes."

Wentworth shook his head. "You miss the idea, Kirk. I have no intention of escaping detection. I shall invite it! The point is that in such a case, an imposture like that, the underlings would have to communicate with the Wreck. That is our trouble now. We can find no trail that leads us even approximately to the Wreck, though we can find a thousand presumptive underlings. Therefore, we must make the trail ourselves!"

Kirkpatrick's haggard blue eyes regarded him unwaveringly through a long minute. "It might work," he muttered, "though I don't know how he could make sure of following the trail once it was established. We can't do anything as open as surround the district. Perhaps something could be worked out... but you're not going to put on the disguise, Dick. It's almost certain death and we need your brains here. I'll call for volunteers."

"And tell your plan to the whole force?"

"That won't be necessary," Kirkpatrick said steadily. "I'll merely say 'for a secret mission in which death is practically certain!'"

"Even at that," Wentworth acknowledged, "I think men would volunteer for you, Kirk. But once more, you miss the point. As you say, it would be practically impossible for any man to follow the trail we created—for any man—*except the impostor!* He will certainly be taken, a prisoner, to the Wreck. Therefore, Kirk, you see this job will call for what you are pleased to designate as my brains, as well as the willingness to die in a hopeless cause! It will also call for ruthless action at the end of the trail!"

Kirkpatrick said, "Damn it, Dick, I won't allow it!"

Wentworth rose steadily to his feet. "You haven't a thing to do with it, Kirk! You can cooperate if you wish, throw up a few safeguards, but you can't keep me from doing it by anything less than arrest. And even that won't detain me for long. You understand? I'm going!"

Kirkpatrick said, "No, Dick." There was a revolver suddenly in his hand and he rose firmly behind his desk. "A bullet through the leg won't stop your brain from working, but it will put an end to this foolishness. I want your promise to drop this mad idea."

ACROSS THE expanse of the desk, the two friends confronted each other with grim and angry faces. They were strangely alike in the strength of their profiles, in the stalwart, reliant carriage of their bodies—alike, too, in their honesty of purpose. Wentworth knew that Kirkpatrick was determined to shoot if necessary. The gun was held as unwaveringly as the frosty regard of the commissioner's blue eyes.

"This is madness, Kirk," Wentworth urged. "Even our combined efforts have been insufficient to check the Wreck. If we quarrel…."

"There will be no quarrel," Kirkpatrick told him grimly. "This once, you will take my orders!"

The affection he always felt for this severe man warmed Wentworth's heart. He knew that it was more their mutual regard that prompted Kirkpatrick to this course, the fear that he might be killed in such a hazardous undertaking, than any great immediate need for his counsel. And it was a thing which the Spider must do! None of his understanding showed in Wentworth's face. Instead, it became distorted with an anger that he never allowed himself to evince. He beat the desk with his clenched fist.

"Confound it, Kirkpatrick," he said furiously, "you're overstepping yourself! I take orders from no man!"

"Nevertheless," Kirkpatrick returned stolidly, "this time you will!"

"Never!" Wentworth flung at him, and slammed his fist down

hard again—and this time very accurately upon the edge of a large concave ashtray! It was beautifully calculated and the whole copper bowl flipped into the air straight for Kirkpatrick's face! The lighter ashes flew before it, blinded him. In a single stride, Wentworth was around the desk.

"Sorry, Kirk," he muttered—and swung accurately for the jaw!

He caught the commissioner as he slumped forward, unconscious, and eased him to the floor. Wentworth's eyes were gentle. Had he been less sure of his friend, he could never have taken that risk, but he knew that Kirkpatrick would not fire when there was danger of hurting him seriously.

Swiftly then, Wentworth scoured Kirkpatrick's desk and found the notation on the location of the lodging-houses. He could not leave that here lest Kirk should raid them to protect him. A moment he lingered over his friend, then he strode from the office.

"The commissioner doesn't wish to be disturbed until he signals," Wentworth told the secretary in the outer office before he hurried out of the building. His plans already were made. He would speed to his forlorn home and transform himself into the Wreck. He had just time before darkness fell. Then straight to the lodging houses… He switched on his radio and tuned in police calls. He reflected with a faint smile that Kirkpatrick might well have him arrested for assault!

Wentworth was prepared for that, but the news that came over the radio shocked him inexpressibly He stared incredulously at the instrument and afterward drove on, blindly, his mind refusing to accept the thing he heard. "Calling all cars," the announcer said in a clipped, angry voice. "Calling all cars. General alarm. Pick up Richard Wentworth on suspicion of attempted murder. He is armed and dangerous!" The man went on with the description of Wentworth and the Hispano he was driving, then the voice lost the impersonal drawl into which it had dropped. Wentworth was the last man seen with Commissioner Kirkpatrick. The Commissioner was shot and is in a critical condition! He is unconscious! Take no chances, men."

Wentworth shook his head violently. This didn't make sense… Unless Kirkpatrick was framing him temporarily to get him into custody? No, no, there could be no mistaking the vehemence of the announcer. And Kirkpatrick would not issue an order which the police would be sure to interpret as a "shoot to kill" order! And that was what the announcer meant….

"He is armed and dangerous. Take no chances…."

Wentworth's jaw locked grimly. This meant that the Wreck had at last succeeded in an attempt to remove Kirkpatrick! And he, Richard Wentworth, had helped the Wreck… by knocking out his friend. By the heavens, he would press his plan through to an immediate conclusion. Let them capture him in the disguise of the Wreck. They would regret the day… but he would have to abandon his house until Kirkpatrick could revive and tell the truth… if he ever did revive! There were things in his home he needed; money from the cash supply he always kept, articles of make-up… Once he had those. Richard Wentworth must disappear!

He must….

With a whine, the police radio broke in again on his thoughts.

"Cars Two-thirty-one, Two-thirty-four, Two-thirty-seven, Cruiser Seven, proceed with all speed to Sutton Place! Wentworth believed proceeding to his home. Enter the home by force, if necessary, and await him there! Report as soon as possible."

It ended.

Wentworth swore harshly. If he could beat the cars there… Abruptly, his eyes whipped to the rear-vision mirror. Bearing down on him, in ominous silence, and at terrific speed, was a police radio car! He heard the thin wailing of other sirens as the officers rushed toward his home. His foot drove on the accelerator and the Hispano leaped ahead, swerved westward around the next corner with the tires shrieking wildly. The radio car was just behind. Even as he made the corner, he saw the roof-slide of the car open and a policeman thrust up his head and drew out a rifle.

Wentworth's lips were set in a thin, fierce line. The Wreck had contrived a master stroke! From now on, the Spider must fight the police as well as the underworld. Abruptly, Wentworth stood on the brake! Into the other end of the street, another police car was whirling. A rifle bullet cracked past his head and punched through the windshield. He was trapped!

From now on, he had thought. He would be more than fortunate if he survived the next two minutes!

CHAPTER 7
IN THE ENEMY HANDS

THERE WAS no hope of escaping the police pursuit in his swift car. Both ends of the narrow street were plugged physically by radio coupés. His Hispano might possibly drive one aside, but meantime in his unarmored car, he would be riddled with police bullets. He was out of his own machine even while the thought crossed his mind and, diving away from the pursuing whine of rifle lead, hurled himself in between two parked sedans.

It was a temporary refuge and he leaped for the doorway of a small apartment house. He made the lobby, but the inner portal barred his way. No time to fool with buzzing an apartment so that someone would operate the electrical release of the lock… His gun leaped to his hand and he smashed its butt through the plate glass, reached through to twist the knob.

The police were close behind. He heard the beat of their feet upon the pavement, their eager shouts. He swung down a flight of steps and found himself in a close-walled cement court. There were only two exits—the one by which he had entered and the locked gate which gave on the street from which he had just fled. He raced, soft-footed, to the gate. There would be guards in the street and he must give them warning by shooting off the padlock. No help for it. The automatic jarred against his hand and his shoulder, driving into the gate, hurled it wide.

He caught a glimpse of a single man in police uniform at the entrance of the apartment, saw the man's face turn white, his eyes widen as he clawed for his service revolver. Wentworth fanned a bullet over his head and the man's first shot went wild as he dodged. An instant later, Wentworth flung himself back into his own roadster and kicked the starter. The engine caught and the Hispano was rolling in the same instant. He threw a quick look ahead, set the course of the car and locked the wheel there with rigidly set wrists, flung himself prone on the cushions.

The policeman's gun and whistle were going crazy behind him. Bullets slammed into the body of the Hispano or whined overhead. Then Wentworth's left fender clanged violently against a parked car. He wrenched the wheel a fraction over and heard the metal rip free. He risked a quick poke with one hand and whipped the rear-vision mirror down so that it gave a partial view of the street ahead. It was easier now. He wrenched at the hand throttle and the gun-sounds dropped behind.

The accentuated shouts told him that the police who had entered the apartment building were back on his trail again. Only one thing to do and, calmly, Wentworth prepared. Fifty more feet would bring him to the corner. He drove half that distance with mounting speed, then whipped the wheel hard over. The Hispano nudged into the cars on the left of the street and the rear end slewed around, blocking the narrow passage between parked machines. Wentworth used the surge of that double impact to slide him across the car, batted open the door and was instantly out and running again at top speed.

He ducked around the corner into Lexington, popped into a taxi and waved a ten-dollar bill at the driver with his left hand. His right presented his automatic.

"Take your choice," Wentworth said coolly, "but drive fast."

The driver was a youngster who wore thick glasses. His eyes popped behind them and the engine howled as he whipped out into the traffic. The cab was turning a corner a block away when the police poured, on foot, into Lexington. Wentworth glimpsed them springing toward another cab and, out of sight, flung the ten-dollar bill to the seat beside the driver.

"Slow down," he said, "then get away fast. If I were you, I'd get where the cops won't have a chance to talk to you. They're apt to be sore."

The boy stammered, "Y-yes, sir. I'll get away."

He kicked his brake and Wentworth hit the pavement running while the cab roared on. He was crouched out of sight in a dark doorway when the cops rounded the corner in two other taxis a few moments later... by which time the young taxi driver was ducking out of sight a block away. When the police had slammed past and were gone, Wentworth crept out of hiding and paced unhurriedly back to Lexington. His face was clear, unworried, but there was turmoil within him. One by one, the Wreck stripped his friends from him. Kirkpatrick shot, and critically wounded; the rest... God alone knew what was happening to Nita....

WENTWORTH DARED not risk another taxi from this neighborhood. He had to break the trail, permanently. From this moment, Richard Wentworth must disappear. A subway train sped him southward and later he walked rapidly through dark side streets toward one of the three small garages around the city in which he had parked his deceptively battered coupés and their caches of make-up. He would not lack for guns and ammunition, but his cash was running low and now there would be no opportunity to refurnish his purse. His bank accounts undoubtedly would be watched... Well, his enemies should supply his needs!

He pitched headlong down the
steps—a crutch hurled after him!

Once the garage was reached, Wentworth set rapidly to work. Under the deft manipulations of his hands, the polished clubman rapidly vanished and the face became haggard and gouged by chronic pain. He created hollows in his throat so that it seemed thin and corded and artificial brows made his eyes sunken and small. He hesitated over making a fake hump for his back. He could hunch his shoulders to give the appearance of being crippled, and the contrivance might hamper him

when the need came for swift action... He shook his head. No, he must have the false hump. The imposture must be as accurate as possible.

He rapidly formed a cage out of lengths of stiff wire, padded it with cloth and strapped it to his shoulders... and presently he drew over it the Spider's cape. Fortunate that the Wreck had chosen for himself a costume similar to that assumed by the Spider. That much of his task was simplified. A wig, a slouch hat... Wentworth surveyed himself as well as possible by the small mirror. He shambled back and forth across the garage and his head, dangling before the false hump, took on quick, bird-like movements. For a few moments, he practiced the rasping mockery of the Wreck's voice, then he was ready. What could be done by a skillful man to imitate the Wreck had been done. He was prepared for his invasion of the stronghold of the Monster Men.

Swiftly, Wentworth backed the coupé from the garage and waited while the automatic mechanism swung the doors shut again. Then he tooled cautiously from the alleyway. A wry smile touched his lips. It was a grim mockery that he was safer thus in the disguise of the Wreck than in his own identity. In this guise, he had only the police to fight. Both underworld and the law were hounding Richard Wentworth!

Wentworth had no illusions about the ease or safety of what he was about to attempt. It was a desperate last resort in which he might succeed in locating the Wreck—but would be more than apt to forfeit his life! The wounding of Kirkpatrick, and his removal from control of the police had reduced his chances by seventy-five percent. But there was no wavering of Richard Wentworth's firm resolve, no slackening of his calm courage. Before this, the Spider had fought single-handed against the forces of crime and evil.

Deliberately, Wentworth built up his own morale, but the fact that conscious effort was necessary told more plainly than any words that he knew himself to be shaken and unsure of himself.

Never before had he fought so long with so few actual accomplishments against an enemy; never before had his best strategy turned only to mockery and chagrin. The dark desertion of the streets of this gala capital of the world gave ample testimony to the Wreck's successes. Wentworth forced himself to the realization that the Wreck, without doubt, was the cleverest and most ruthless criminal who ever had risen to control of the underworld!

The cripples' dormitory toward which Wentworth sped was a dilapidated tenement building within sound of the rush and roar of the New York Central trains where they racketed out of their tunnel beneath city streets and mounted the stilts of an elevated structure. Wentworth had spotted it this same day by the simple expedient of trailing a cripple throughout the long hours of his begging tour about the city. He parked his coupé a block away and shambled with his cripple's gait into another doorway a dozen houses away, then mounted its creaking stairways to the roof.

From this vantage point, he peered down into the street to make a final reconnoiter. His eyes narrowed at sight of a bedraggled wagon, drawn by a boneyard horse, that stood before the dormitory building. The wagon was heaped high with a miscellaneous collection of junk and papers and, as he watched, a cripple laboriously climbed up the basement stairs to deposit further piles of refuse upon the walk. For an instant, Wentworth's certainties wavered.

Was it possible that the cripple he had followed through so many hours was just what he appeared, a beggar who eked out a meager living by panhandling and collecting junk from the city's trash cans? Well, he would soon resolve that question! Wentworth turned back from the roof's edge and hurried toward the kiosk that marked the entrance to the cripple dormitory. At the door, Wentworth paused. Briefly, he touched the automatics that nestled beneath his arms, shrugged to make sure of the purchase of the artificial hump up on his shoulders. Then he drew his robe about him, and opened the door.

UTTER BLANK darkness lay beneath him as fetid close air pushed up against his face. The only sound that reached his ears was the whimpering snore of a man. It rose and fell in regular cadences. Wentworth closed the door behind him and passed with quiet stealth down the steps. They uttered no complaint under his practiced feet. He passed the door of the snorer, pushed on.

Dim light from a specked bulb filtered up toward him now and, when he had descended another flight, he could hear the distant mumble of voices. That faint bell-note, repeated irregularly, meant that the junk wagon was moving on. Wentworth put that out of his immediate thoughts. Presently, he would seek the meaning of that junk wagon, but now all his faculties were concentrated on the task ahead.

The mumble of voices he traced to a doorway beneath which a splinter of brilliant white light pushed out. He checked just outside it, caught the dully muttered argot of a game of poker. From the sound, he judged that some seven or eight men were in that close room. Even here in the hall, the stale stench of tobacco smoke was heavy and laid a faint blue haze upon the air.

He hesitated, then pushed on. He wanted the leader, the man in charge of this dormitory. He doubted that he would find the man in the game. Usually, the leader had his quarters either on the first floor or in the basement. If it were in the cellar story here, that junk might have some further significance! Wentworth was half-way down the final flight to the first floor when light blazed brilliantly in the hallway. He heard a stifled cry and two men were peering up at him with frightened eyes.

"Out with that light, fool," Wentworth snarled in the rasping accents of the Wreck. "Do you want me seen from the street?"

"Yes, master," one of the men mumbled "I mean, no, master. I…" He switched off the light and by contrast the dimness of the previous illumination was like pitch darkness.

Wentworth let a slight smile of triumph cross his lips. That brilliant light would quickly expose his make-up… and by the promptness of obedience he knew that for the present he had convinced the men below of his identity. He peered down at the two, one of them a one-legged man who stumped along on a single crutch. The other had no visible deforming. On previous raids, the police always had found the leader uncrippled, so it was the latter whom Wentworth addressed.

"Have you got my instructions, fool?" he demanded, and his rasping tones were precisely those of the Wreck; so was the reptilian forward thrust of his head. His hunched shadow created a monster on the wall. "Well, fool, why don't you answer? Or perhaps you gentlemen have lost your tongues? It is an idea, losing your tongues—an idea I have not yet developed...."

"Yes, master," the leader hurried. "I have your instructions, but they were just delivered. I haven't had time…" He was fumbling some papers from an inside pocket. "You must pardon me, master. I did not know you were here, and it… you startled me."

Wentworth snorted. "A fine watch you keep over this house. Quickly, fool, the papers!"

The man started up the stairs, yet checked three steps below Wentworth's distorted figure. "Of course, sir, certainly, sir. Please, master, you won't blame me for being cautious, but with your own lips you told me never to obey an order of yours unless you accompanied it by the… *the word!* You won't mind my asking you for the word?"

An oath leaped to Wentworth's lips, even while his mind grinned mockingly at him. Checkmate in the instant of triumph! Those instructions would undoubtedly detail some robbery, or some kidnapping raid. Possession of them might perhaps enable him to catch important men of the Wreck, a much better chance than that he was attempting here… and it would permit him, too, to thwart the Wreck's plans!

"You quibble with me, I think, my fool," he said softly. "It appears you have found your tongue at last, and too well. Yes, quite a bit too well."

He snatched the papers from the man's hand, fumbled them open. "Yes, yes, these are the right ones," he muttered, while his narrowed eyes raced over the words in the dim light of the hall.

The instructions were simple and direct: "Have your full force at the emergency subway exit at Third Avenue and Seventy first Street at precisely 9:03 in the morning." It was signed *The Wreck*.

But the leader was still speaking, "Master, you must give me the countersign. You yourself insisted that I should ask for it. Why do you withhold it now?"

"Pah, don't bother me," Wentworth snarled, and stumped down the steps toward the man. In the hallway below, the one-legged cripple was watching with a tension that drew his upward strained throat into cords. To Wentworth, he seemed the more dangerous of the two men, and danger was a thing he must estimate narrowly now.

Previously, it had been his deliberate intention to betray his imposture, but that no longer was the wiser move. He must escape, must give warning... His lips thinned with pressure. God help him, it was plain enough, wasn't it? The Wreck was planning another slave raid! He was going to kidnap a train full of people in the subway rush hour! The emergency exit... Yes, that was obvious.

His thoughts were a thing apart from Wentworth's actions. He kept up a mumbling tirade. "Countersign," he rasped. "Countersign indeed! You, my fine fool, do not even remember the countersign! Repeat it to me, privately in my ear, fool. Let me hear...."

What he heard was a shrill shout from the cripple below, "Hey! Hey, that ain't the Wreck! He's a fake. I can tell...."

Scarcely had the words started to spill from the man's lips when the leader piped on a shrill whistle almost in Wentworth's ear and a savage blow caught Wentworth on the base of the skull.

He pitched headlong down the steps, caught at the railing with a frantic hand while his other fist clawed for his automatic. It ripped free of the holster but he was still off-balance, half-falling, half running down the steep, creaking stairs. The cripple whipped his crutch through the air like a javelin and Wentworth flung himself aside just in time.

It cost him his scant hold on the railing and he plunged down, trying to catch himself while that whistle raised hell above him. Dazzling light was smashing down into the hallway. Wentworth missed the bottom step and sprawled full-length in the lower hall. He rolled, whipping up his gun... and there was a rattling clatter on the stairs, a dragging, thumping sound of crippled men who flung themselves frantically to the attack. Wentworth's gun swung into line, blasted.

His bullet caught a man already in mid-leap and he saw the dying twitch of the extended limbs, silhouetted blackly against the dazzle of the lights. The body slammed down against his chest and while he fought it aside, fought to bring his gun once more into line, another and another shock beat down upon his recumbent body. It must have been the butt end of a crutch that found his skull. It seemed to drive in through the bone with the viciousness of the thrust. Wentworth knew an instant of agonizing pain; then he knew nothing at all….

WHEN WENTWORTH fought his way back to consciousness, it was with the realization that hours must have passed since the attack on the steps. He could hear the rapid hollow rapping of many feet passing somewhere near, and the raucous rising bleat of a snore. Cautiously, before he opened his eyes, he moved hands and feet and discovered that they had been painfully bound. There was a pounding agony through his brain whose throbbing almost blotted out the possibility of thought… until he remembered the task he must perform.

He forced open his eyes then and dim gray daylight, slitting in through high dusty windows, assaulted them. He understood now that hurrying beat of feet. He was imprisoned in a cellar and what he heard was the rush-hour crowd on its way to work. The rush hour… Good God, if people already were on their way to work, he had indeed been out for hours. It was almost time for the Wreck to strike, to execute his slave raid upon the people of the subway trains, and he… he alone who could warn the police in time! He strained frantically at his bonds and only felt the numb agony of his head, and the stab of pain in his wrists. A dozen feet away, a cripple guard slumbered with a gun in his fist.

Grimly, Wentworth estimated his chances and began to worm on his belly toward the sleeping man. One chance in a dozen that he could reach the man without awakening him; one in a hundred that he would be able to overpower him, bound as he was, and escape. And after that… what were his chances of averting the slave raid? He could not calculate them, but he knew that he, and he alone, stood between the work-bound rush-hour crowds and the raiders of the Wreck!

CHAPTER 8
SLAVE RAID

THE CROWD felt safe in the subway. Jammed into cars by the thrusting shoulders of the platform guards, wedged immovably against each other, they swayed against the lurching of the speeding train—and felt safe.

Terror ruled the city streets these days and no man, certainly no woman, moved alone if he could avoid it. Even parties of two and three had disappeared and never been heard of again. The newspapers were full of these vanishings. But surely here, with hundreds of persons about, they were safe! Despite the early intense heat of the day, the passengers joyed in the close-pressed ranks about them. Down here, too, there were no cripples... They didn't know, these people, that some of the Wreck's slaves were not cripples.

Even when the train slid to a halt between stations and remained motionless with the air compressors throbbing, the crowd did not at first become restless. After all, it was the rush hour and things like this happened. It was simply that the train ahead was slow in unloading its passengers and the signal blocks had turned red.

True, after a few minutes of waiting, people began to stir uneasily. They were thinking that they would be late to their jobs. Even with terror abroad in the city, they didn't think of anything worse than that—not at first... No one noticed that one man moved close to the uniformed subway guard and took a stand behind him, nor saw him ease a gun from his pocket. But then, the crowd could see only what was happening right around them. They couldn't know that every subway guard had a gunman behind him... and still the train was motionless and the silence and the heat began to eat into people's nerves. A man yelled a question and it was caught up, repeated, until voices hammered through the close tunnel of the subway. It was at this moment that the gunman thrust his gun into the guard's back.

"Open the doors," he ordered coldly.

The guard twisted about a strained, suddenly frightened face and the muzzle of the gun dug into his spine. The guard's lips quivered and he put his fingers on the buttons that released air and opened the doors. The gunmen behind him called out, piercingly.

"There's an emergency exit toward the rear of the train," he said.

Men in subway uniforms were suddenly beside the open doors. "Emergency exit to the rear," they called. "File out quietly please. There's no danger, just a block up ahead. Go out the emergency exit. Trucks and buses are waiting to carry you to your destination. Quietly, please. There's no danger."

The crowd began to laugh and their eyes were excited. It was a break in the even routine of the groove that led to and from their offices. Something to talk about. No one could blame them if they did not guess that the Wreck's slave raiders were at work, if they did not guess the fearful change that would take place in their lives—and their bodies!

There was some jostling on the narrow platform beside the cars but the guards dealt strictly with that, and the crowd was for the most part orderly and amused, rather than worried. A legitimate reason to be late at the office, one that the boss would have to accept. It would be in all the papers.

A red light burned at the emergency exit stairs and the people began to file up rapidly. At the surface, the gratings had been opened and a bus was pulled up at the curb. More uniformed men were speeding them across the walk and into the bus, packing it full of human beings, sending it rolling swiftly away. It was a strange thing that all the windows of the buses should be tightly closed in this weather; that they should resist all efforts to open them.

The bus had traveled two blocks before someone noticed that the driver wore a gas mask… When he shouted and tried to stumble toward the door, the man who discovered it felt weakness pulling at all his muscles. His voice scarcely pushed beyond his lips and he clung to a strap, panting, trying to tell the man next to him about the bus driver and the curious mask he wore. It was perhaps thirty seconds later that the first man slumped sideways and sagged to the floor.

It alarmed a few people. They thought he had fainted. Before they could do more than call out excitedly, other people were dropping all around them. Another block, and the bus carried a cargo of unconscious human beings. The only person who stirred was the masked bus driver, and the windows of the bus were

114

curiously fogged. It would be hard for anyone to see inside... The sign on the front read: *Chartered*. It did not read: *Destination: Hell*. It should have....

SIX BLOCKS north and two east of that emergency exit a battered coupé was roaring through the city streets. A grim faced man in nondescript clothing bent tautly over the wheel and on the seat beside him was a revolver. There was a bloody smear on the man's forehead and there was blood, too, on his wrists as if he had ripped them by main force from imprisoning ropes. His eyes were at once desperate and cold with menace. At a corner, he whipped the car in hard to the curb and hit the pavement running; plunged into a drugstore and found a phone booth. His hand clenched with the effort to remain there quietly while his call went through. He knew the time now, and it was fifteen minutes past the time when the raid on the subway was to begin.

"Police headquarters? Connect me with the commissioner... at once." His lips twisted, and he laughed flatly into the mouthpiece. "Yes, you may have my name. Just say—*the Spider is coming!*"

They would trace the call at once, Wentworth knew. Police cars would be rushed to the spot. That was all right, it was the way he wanted it. At least, he would have some police behind him when he dashed into the battle at the emergency exit. He wondered who was in charge of the police in the absence of Kirkpatrick. Probably Milhauser, a good cop but unimaginative....

"Commissioner?" Wentworth snapped.

"The Wreck is raiding a subway train at Seventy-First and

115

Third Avenue. Emergency exit. He's kidnapping a whole train full of people. Get your men there fast or it will be too late. This is the Spider warning you. Hurry, man. Or thousands more will be made into cripples."

He dropped the receiver, left it hanging while he darted from the shop. He wanted the police to have every help in tracing the call! The druggist stared after him as he raced from the shop. It did not matter. Wentworth still wore the facial disguise of the Wreck, though his clothing was that of the man who had been left to guard him. It had been simple, after all, to wriggle close enough to drive his bound feet against the man's jaw and find a knife in the man's pocket. Comparatively simple... but it had taken time. And he was late.

Once more, he sent the coupé roaring southward. Now, as he drove, he drew about his shoulders once more the cape of the Wreck, dragged the black slouch hat down over his brows. He had a double plan. If he failed to stop the slave raid in the garb of the Wreck, then he would discard it and become one of the captured slaves! Before this day was over, he would join battle with the Wreck himself!

Sirens were ripping the air behind him not yet in chase, but near enough to be heard by the subway crowds and the men of the Wreck. That was what he wanted.

He saw a bus with fogged windows humming toward him and, through difficult glass, he saw that the driver wore a gas mask. Wentworth's lips twisted grimly.

It all made sense, didn't it? An emergency exit, and buses to transfer the passengers from the subway train, closed windows and gas. Wentworth caught up the revolver from the seat beside him and sped one careful shot.

The windshield of the bus showed a sudden silvery star. The gas-masked driver wrenched backward in his seat, both arms flung high… and the bus jerked to a halt with a release of emergency air. Wentworth nodded happily as he raced on. All passenger buses these days were equipped with "dead man" throttles that stopped the bus when the driver released his grip. His exultation was short-lived. An instant after he fired, a sedan swerved out from behind the bus and guns began to slant their lurid venomous flames toward his car!

Wentworth clenched his revolver and a challenging grin bared his teeth, but only for a moment. He lowered the gun while bullets hammered against the heavy metal sides of the coupé and ground the accelerator to the floor. He could not lose time here merely to account for a few of the Wreck's underlings. Besides, there were only four bullets left in the chamber of this captured gun and his own weapons had been taken while he was unconscious. He might have graver need of those four bullets later on!

Lead beat on his car like a flurry of rain. A few spattered, frosted spots sprung into sight on his bullet-proof windshield and then he was past. The coupé heeled wildly over as he whipped it across traffic into a side street toward Third Avenue.

Faster….

INSTANTLY, A line of buses sprang into view. They were motionless on Third Avenue and empty—waiting for slaves. Wentworth flung a swift look behind him. He was not pursued, and the siren shriek was closer. The Wreck's guards for the bus would soon have their hands full with the police. Once more, Wentworth whipped his car to the curb and darted into a confectionery store to phone the police. He could not guess how many bus-loads of slaves had been carried away, but if the police stopped all that were labeled *Chartered* and which were driven by gas-masked men....

He flung the information in swift sentences at the acting commissioner of police and darted back to his car. Kirkpatrick, he knew, would have acted instantly at his call. No matter how hard he hunted the Spider, he had learned, through many battles, to trust his information. This new chief was a different matter. If he waited to check on the Spider's message it would be too late.

Wentworth was racing beside the stationary buses now, and he could see the crowd eddying out of the subway exit. They seemed passive, unalarmed. Men in uniform stood about, directing them. Another bus was filled, the doors closed and it lurched forward. Wentworth cut in sharply ahead of it and heard his fenders crumple in the collision, was thrown sideways against the left door as he fumbled for the catch. He pitched out on the pavement, caught himself and shambled toward the guards. Once more, it was the Wreck with out-thrust head and hunched, crippled back who moved; it was the Wreck's rasping, mocking voice that called to them.

"Well done, gentlemen," he cried, "but the pressure grows a bit too strong. The police will be here in a moment. Scatter at once. Back to your holes, rats."

The waiting crowd of huddled humanity from the subway

stared at him motionless until a woman's shrill scream lifted. "Kidnapped! We're being kidnapped!"

Panic burst in that same instant. Men and women broke wildly against the loosely held lines of the men in the garb of subway guards. Above the shouts of terror, another voice lifted shrilly. "That's not the Wreck! He's a fake! Kill him!"

A gun blasted and Wentworth felt lead pluck at the cape that swirled from his shoulders. Instantly, guns sprang to a dozen hands, and out of surrounding buildings a horde of cripples poured! Wentworth made no attempt to battle the small army of killers. He had accomplished a part of his purpose. He whirled and ducked behind his car, the cape billowing from his shoulders. Lead slashed the air behind him. The roll of gunfire filled the street, drowned out even the shrillness of fear in the voices of fleeing men and women.

Wentworth flung a swift glance behind him. As yet, no one of his pursuers was in sight. He flung himself flat on the ground and rolled beneath the bus he had stalled. The instant he was clear of the wheels, its motor roared with the powerful surge of the engine and it began to crush forward against his coupé!

Wentworth reached up and seized the under-bracings of the bus chassis, hooked a knee over a cross-member. He heard the groaning rip of crushing metal, heard a tire on his coupé explode... then the bus surged forward, free of the obstacle. A few feet away, the motor thundered with power, rasped through gear shifts and the bus was underway. A grim smile twisted the set face of Richard Wentworth. If he could secure himself here, he would accomplish the second part of his plan, which was to follow to the hideout of the Wreck himself!

Within inches of his back, the pavement of the street slid past beneath him and his grip on the under-structure was precarious. Let a foot or hand slip and he would be instantly crushed under the heavy tires. If he escaped that, he would be battered and broken when the low swung rear ground over him. But Wentworth did not consider those things. The Spider was on the trail and there would be no swerving!

Laboriously, he set about making a hammock of his cape and the length of silken rope he always carried. It was incredibly difficult, for he must cling with a looped arm and knees while he worked. A hard bump flung his head against a steel cross-beam and his senses reeled. He clung desperately, felt his finger slipping. Frantically, he knotted a loop of the rope, already drawn taut, about his chest.

He felt his body relaxing. A foot bounced on the pavement and his shoe was torn off. He thrust it upward painfully. With every shred of fading consciousness, with every reflex of his maltreated body, he hung on while darkness swirled in his brain. He felt a hand slip and there was no strength in him to tighten that grip!

CHAPTER 9
CRIPPLE FACTORY

A N ETERNITY passed while Wentworth dangled in a stupor beneath the bus. Gradually, the thrust of swift air drew him back to full consciousness. His hands had long ago lost their grip on the steel, but his feet, twisted into an angle between two beams held excruciatingly. It was the rope about his chest that had saved him within a brief inch of dragging on the concrete pavement that now flowed backward beneath him.

It was minutes before he could resume the task of making his position more secure, but at last he contrived a hammock of the rope. It was while he was at work at this that he found the cape had been torn from his shoulders and lay somewhere on the road behind. His hat was gone, too, but the revolver was still secure in his waistband, cramped against his stomach muscles. Nothing now to do save wait while the bus bored on toward the slave camp of the Wreck; wait and try to make plans to rescue these trapped human beings and destroy the Wreck. Meantime, he endeavored to relax in the grip of the thin ropes of the hammock, to gather his strength for the battle that lay ahead.

Wentworth calculated that three conscious hours had passed when finally the bus swung with a lurch from the concrete road and began to crunch over gravel. Bits of stone bombarded him and hammered against the fenders. The bus engine began to howl in low gear, climbing slowly up a steep grade.

Wentworth twisted about in the web he had spun for himself and peered ahead. Under the low structure of the bus, he could see only a short distance of the gravel road ahead, but they were climbing. When they crested the hill he should be able to catch a brief glimpse of what lay ahead. He thought they were nearing the sanitarium from which the Wreck sent his floods of cripples upon the city, but he could not be sure. Nor could he risk an attack while uncertain.

The bus labored more strenuously and Wentworth's hopes mounted. A sharp rise would give him better perspective when… He muffled a cry as the bus topped the hill and he caught a brief glimpse of a valley beyond. On the rise of the hill beyond, back under the trees where it would be hard to spot from overhead, was a long white building, toward which the narrow road twisted. It was only for an instant that Wentworth could see the building, then the nose of the bus dropped and he spotted the close-growing trees in the bottom below, the sharp rise beyond.

A slow, taut smile moved Wentworth's lips and, carefully, he eased the revolver into his hand. He glanced at the hammock in which he lay. He had been more intent on making it secure than on providing easy egress, but it would not be too difficult. He slid out the pocket-knife taken from the cripple guard he had overpowered long ago, opened it and gripped it between his teeth.

The bus was swooping down the grade, roaring dangerously on the narrow road. The hammer of gravel against the fenders was like a series of pistol shots. The bottom flashed past, the bus slammed into a lower gear. Wentworth twisted about once more, leveled the revolver carefully… and shot the right front tire off the bus!

Blast of gun and exploding tire formed one concurrent sound and the bus lurched crazily toward the ditch. Wentworth's lips were tight. He knew what the ditch was like. If the bus slewed one set of wheels into it, the ridge of the road's edge would crush him to a pulp against the bottom of the bus. No time to think about that. He was at work on the silken skeins of his hammock, slashing through them with his knife.

The wrecked front tire slipped off the road, lurched heavily as the bus skidded toward the ditch. Wentworth's lips tore apart in a soundless cry. He slashed twice more at the silken skeins, then as the rear wheel followed the front into the ditch, he flung himself to the gravel road, rolling frantically.

The bus was still traveling forward and the giant double rear wheel crunched the gravel toward Wentworth as he rolled. He jerked his feet out of the way just in time, doubled his body frantically, clawed with his hands. The wheel was right on top of him. He felt the pinch of it on the tail of his coat. He was caught, caught....

He wriggled his arms free of the coat and, suddenly, could move no farther. He felt strain upon his shoulders and for whole seconds could not understand why. Then he realized the tire of the bus had become stationary upon the artificial hump he had strapped to his back to simulate the Wreck's deformity....

HE HEARD the swish of air as a door of the bus opened. Fortunately, he was on the left hand side. He had calculated on that when deliberately he had shot off the right front tire. Now it had saved his life. He struggled with the straps that held the wire cage upon his shoulders. When he staggered to his feet, he was naked to the waist. There were red ridges across his shoulders where the bits of wire had gouged into the flesh. His legs and arms felt uncertain, wooden, after the long strain of that trip and there was a numbness in his brain. He needed no thought for the thing he was about to do.

Beyond the high hood of the bus, he could hear the swearing of the bus driver as he inspected the wreckage of the tire. Wentworth set his foot upon the hub of the near wheel. In two quick steps, he had mounted the top of the hood—and hurled himself through the air at the bus driver!

The man glimpsed Wentworth when he was in mid-flight. He pushed himself backward, snatched for a shoulder gun. He was going backward when Wentworth's shoulder hit his chest, pinned him breathless against the grass bank across the ditch. But the man's gun had come free. He twisted his wrist to bring it to bear on Wentworth and the Spider's own revolver traveled in a crisp arc that terminated just above the man's left ear. Under that blow, the driver jerked and went limp.

Wentworth staggered to his feet and threw a quick look at the bus. Both doors were open and the hot sweet air of June was circulating through it readily. If the prisoners could be revived by anything less than medication, that would accomplish it! Wentworth bent again over the bus driver. He strapped the man's leather puttees on over his own trousers, stripped off the gray shirt and uniform cap and rapidly donned them. The gas mask, he caught up off the grass but the real treasure was the man's short-barreled revolver with a dozen extra rounds of ammunition. Wentworth weighed that lovingly in his hand as he straightened from his work.

Not until then was he aware of the breathless quiet of the summer day and the scent of the bruised grass about him. In the hedge, a cicada shrilled its racketing song and from a distance a rooster lifted a mournful challenge—and up on the hill, the Wreck was waiting for his prey!

Wentworth bent grimly over the bus driver once more and bound him with the man's own belt, then hauled him to the door of the bus and heaved him inside. He waited outside long enough to adjust the gas mask over his own face, then followed.

No more than five minutes had elapsed since he had blown out the bus tire. How much more time did he have? Probably, his was the last bus to leave the city. He had precipitated a gun battle into which the police would be plunging within moments of his departure. Whatever else the men of the Wreck had done, there wouldn't have been the opportunity for seizing more slaves. No, the only chance that there might be others behind him would be that some of the gunmen had orders to follow the last bus. That was what he must risk.

He started up the heavy motor of the bus and, after a few minutes of effort, succeeded in running it out of the ditch. He alighted then to gather up his coat and vest from the ground, transferred various objects to the pockets of his captured uniform. Still no sign of any farther arrivals, nor any indication that those at the sanitarium knew that anything was amiss with the bus. Fortunately, he was out of sight of the place.

He climbed back in and surveyed the passengers of the bus, and his eyes lighted with hope as he saw one of the men near the door begin to stir faintly. Wentworth whipped off the gas mask. Others of the passengers were beginning to regain consciousness.

Through ten agonizingly slow minutes, Wentworth waited

while more and more of the men and women came to befuddled consciousness. A few gazed feebly toward him, or made aimless movements to stand, but for the most part they were completely dazed and bewildered. Wentworth began to sting them with words.

"You're safe," he hurled at them. "Safe, if you'll snap out of it and get ready to fight. The Wreck has his fort up on the hill and if we wait much longer he's apt to send men to find out why we're late. Snap out of it, now. Hurry!"

EXCITEMENT BEGAN to sting life into the people, and Wentworth watched a man unfold himself from among a huddle of other prostrate bodies on the floor... and saw that he wore the blue uniform of a policeman! Well, why not? The men of the Wreck would not dare attempt to weed him out from among the rest, and he would make as husky cripple as any other. Wentworth bent over him and took his gun before he was fully conscious. He had to have things completely in control for the present.

Rapidly, Wentworth pushed on with his talk, told the people just what had been done and how... what fate lay ahead of them if they did not follow his orders.

"There is no chance to get this bus away with a punctured tire," he said steadily. "The Wreck and his killers would be after us in a dozen seconds. And there is no chance to escape on foot. But we still have one way we can win."

The cop was fumbling back to full possession of his faculties now. He stared belligerently at Wentworth.

"Say, who are you?" he demanded. "How do we know we can trust you? You may be one of them Wreck men."

Wentworth smiled at him thinly. "If I were one of his men," he said quietly, "I would have delivered you, still unconscious, to the sanitarium on the hill. As to who I am…" He stooped swiftly and pressed the base of a platinum cigarette lighter to the forehead of the unconscious bus driver. Then he wrenched the man to his feet and propped him against a roof support. "There," he said steadily. "Now, you may see who I am."

The whisper that ran through the bus was at once frightened and awed as the eyes of the people centered on the red seal that glowed on the white flesh of the bus driver's forehead—*the seal of the Spider!*

"Up there on the hill," Wentworth said softly, "is the fort of the Wreck. He does not have any men on guard there. No need, for his victims are delivered to him unconscious. That is where he manufactures cripples out of healthy human beings like you… and you… and you." He picked out three able-bodied young men near him, nodded finally to the cop.

"We have so damnably little time to lose. If we go up the hill and he thinks we are all unconscious inside here, there will be no precautions. You can jump the guards he sends for you, get their guns and in a few minutes we will be in charge of the whole sanitarium. Perhaps, we will catch the Wreck himself. If we delay here, his men will come, and we will have no chance. Will you follow the Spider to victory? Or will you become the crippled slaves of the Wreck?"

For a moment, only blank silence answered him. The cop

shifted his footing uncertainly. A woman laughed jerkily. "Are you all cowards?" she asked harshly. "Would you rather be slaves? Spider, you can count on me."

Wentworth smiled toward her, nodded, and there was a rush of assent from the men. The cop frowned, "It's my duty to arrest you, Spider," he said.

Wentworth laughed. "Later on, officer. Just now you are helpless. I have your gun. Now, men, here are the instructions. I will start the bus and drive up the hill to the sanitarium. All doors and windows closed. I've disconnected the gas that knocked you out. The wrecked tire will explain our delay and a certain number of guards will come toward us. We will wait until they are close before we open the doors, then all together! I'll give the word, and lead the way. Are you ready?"

The rumble of assent from the men was chest-deep and sharp with determination. Wentworth nodded, swung into the driver's seat and sent the bus lurching forward. He fitted on the gas mask, and the two guns were tucked into his waistband. Now and again, he glanced back at the crowd behind him. The men were huddled in the aisle, clinging to seat handles and standards. The policeman was among them, but he was making no effort after his gesture at arrest. Perhaps he realized the glory that would come to him if he helped capture the Wreck. Perhaps he feared the Spider....

WENTWORTH KEPT his eyes questing restlessly ahead over the narrow gravel road. The bus lurched and thundered with its bad tire. It was a herculean task to hold it to the driveway, but Wentworth gave it no more than part of his attention. He had painted an easy picture to these men. It was necessary if he hoped for their help at all.

He knew that the brunt of the attack must rest upon himself. He had three guns, though it was true one held only three bullets. If only he dared trust one of these others with a gun... He shook his head. No, he must be the spearhead of the attack. If he could down the first guards, there would be more weapons. What happened afterward must depend on the layout and the number of enemies.

Wentworth frowned, remembering the attack of the cripples in the lodging-house. If there were many cripples at the sanitarium, and they were equally obedient to the Wreck's orders, it would be a difficult battle that lay ahead. The cripples here certainly were not criminals; they were as helpless victims of the Wreck as were these others just arrived by bus in charge of the slave raiders.

Wentworth tensed as he caught sight of a car speeding toward him from the sanitarium, but he did not check his pace. His hand moved briefly to the guns at his waist, then whipped back to the wheel. Probably, they had been sent to see why the bus was delayed after it had been sighted on the crest of that rise from which he himself had first seen the sanitarium. The car stopped in his path with a squeal of brakes and Wentworth stepped on the air, jerked to a halt. One of the men waved a hand at him and he waved back, pointing toward the punctured tire. If they got out and came toward him....

Instead, the car began to back and presently ducked into a narrow roadway, whirled and raced back the way it had come.

Wentworth was aware then that he had been holding his breath, and that the men behind him were taut with fear.

"It will be easy if we strike swiftly," Wentworth said confidently. "We have mostly cripples to fight. Did you notice the men in the car?"

The men in the car had not been cripples, but he needed to encourage his shaky raiders. The bus was laboring up the last long slope toward the sanitarium. Wentworth's poise behind the wheel was easy and undaunted and the men behind him took courage from that fact, but he knew well the dangers of the thing he was about to attempt. He tried to calculate the number of guards who would be stationed at the place.

The building, he could see now, was three stories and close to a hundred feet long. A dozen or a hundred men might be stationed there to protect it. He could only hope that most of them were cripples. Otherwise, defeat and death awaited at the crest of the hill.

Wentworth's lips drew back in a taut smile and his eyes held once more the icy, terrifying stare of the Spider, of him who was known as the Master of Men. He might find death at the crest of the hill but nothing less than that would spell defeat for him or turn him aside from his quest. His goal was fixed: The Wreck... or death.

HE WHEELED the bus out of the cut through which the road had climbed and saw that the way ahead wound through a high steel fence and looped toward the sanitarium around a small bright pond. There were six buses side by side before the building, and a score of men grouped on the verandah included the bus drivers. Beyond them was a huddled mass of cripples who seemed motionless in fear. At least, not one of them moved and Wentworth's eyes shifted back to the score of men who stood on the verandah.

He had hoped there would be fewer, or that the layout would permit him to capture a part of the guard before the rest became alarmed. A frontal attack was impossible with his limited armament and faltering, inexperienced adherents. It would only mean death for many of them, capture for the rest. Nor could he turn the bus aside short of the rank where the others were parked. It would bring the entire squad of men after him in furious haste!

Desperately, his eyes quested over the lawn—surveying pond and road and the narrow trickle of water that formed a small brook across the lawn. His gaze rested for a moment on the culvert that spanned the brook and a thin smile touched his lips. There was just a chance....

"We're in more danger than I thought," he called softly to the men behind him. "Two of you come close to me. Right. I'm going to let the bus go out of control and jump into that ditch. My guess is that when I get out and swear over it only a few of the guard will come down. When they are quite near, you two will show yourselves in the doorway long enough for them to see you. Act as if you were drunk. As soon as they see you, duck back inside. I want everyone else to stretch out as if the gas still had him unconscious. I'll do the rest... But if I call on you to attack, strike with everything you've got and all at once! Understood?"

His eyes flicked to the rear-vision mirror and took in the set faces of the two men behind him. "Right, Spider," one of them said, and grinned suddenly. "We'll play them a neat trick or two."

Wentworth nodded He had to trust the men. It was the only way. He was leaving the major part of the job to himself, and that was as it should be… He loosed the wheel and it whipped suddenly to the right. The bus swerved violently, lurched off the culvert into the ditch and settled.

"All ready, men," Wentworth said quietly as he flung open the door and climbed out from behind the wheel. "Remember, everybody in the bus pretend unconsciousness except you two. Don't give them a chance to shoot you."

He jumped down to the ground. Angrily, he hurled his gas mask to the grass and stood, fists on hips, cursing beside that right front wheel. He heard laughter dimly from the sanitarium, then his slitted eyes saw six men detach themselves and begin to saunter across the grass toward him.

Wentworth drew in a quick breath. So far, so good… but the real danger came when they approached near enough to recognize him.

"Get ready," Wentworth called softly toward the bus. *"Here they come!"*

CHAPTER 10
BATTLE OF THE BUS

WENTWORTH CONTINUED to curse as the guards of the Wreck came toward him in a loose group. But his eyes were secretly on them while he appeared to stare down into the brook where the front wheel of the bus rested. When they had approached so near that he thought he was in danger of being identified by any who knew the real bus driver, he turned his back. He got down on his knees to examine the wheel, to peer under the bus where the front axle rested on the edge of the culvert.

"Where'd you learn how to drive?" one of the men called jeeringly.

"Oh, go to hell!" Wentworth grumbled in his chest. It might have been any man's voice. He poked his head under the front of the bus. From the corner of his eye, he could see that the men were within twenty feet of him. He waited a moment longer, then struck the underside of the chassis violently—the signal agreed upon with the two men in the bus.

"How are your patients?" the same guard jeered.

"Out cold," Wentworth rasped, and began to back out from under the bus.

He was tautly ready. This would call for lightning-fast work. There must not be a single gunshot to alarm the guards at the sanitarium. He glanced toward the building. Thanks to the angle to which the bus had tilted, nothing that went on behind it would be visible up there....

Why in God's name didn't the two men show themselves as he had ordered? In another moment, the guards would recognize him, and then....

A shout behind him jerked Wentworth from under the bus and upright. "Hey, look, punk! Them guys are waking up! Quick!"

Wentworth let out an excited shout and jumped across the

brook toward the entrance of the bus. "Grab them," he shouted. "Don't shoot! There can't be more than one or two of them waking up."

As he leaped, the guards were right behind him. The two men had reeled back from the doorway of the bus, out of sight, and Wentworth felt a lift of hope. So far, things had worked out all right. If he could just maneuver... Leaping, Wentworth's right foot slipped so that he pitched down on hands and knees on the far side of the brook. His feet slipped into the water. He cursed, scrambled, and fell back again. Men were leaping past him toward the door of the bus. Three, four, five! Wentworth's lips were drawn taut against his teeth. His fists closed on the guns at his waist. Just behind him, he caught the thud of a foot as the sixth man took off to jump the brook.

Wentworth's move was lightning fast. He twisted, seized the man's ankle as he flung through the air. There was a muffled, frantic shout, and the man sprawled violently toward the earth. His hands and chest struck together on the farther bank and Wentworth chopped once with a gun to the base of his skull. There was no need to wait and make sure. He knew how he had struck.

A leap took him to the heels of the next man and he swung the gun sideways above the ear. Two down, but there were still four more armed guards and three of them were grouped together, jammed into the doorway of the bus. The fourth had climbed inside.

His two guns poised ready to strike. Wentworth leaped upon the backs of the men in the doorway. The thuds of the barrels against two skulls made a loud sound. Wentworth was aware of the white faces of the two remaining men, twisting toward him, saw the guns glint in their hands as they swung upward. He leaped toward them, but the falling bodies of his two remaining victims were in the way.

"Grab them!" he called, incisively to his men inside the bus. "Grab them quick!"

He heard a muffled shout within the bus and saw the man who had mounted the step twist toward the sound. But the last man was jerking up his gun to fire, and Wentworth knew that he could not reach him in time, could not fire nor allow him to do so. A single shot would bring the entire balance of the force charging down upon him. Frantically, he hurled his right gun at the man's face while he fought to get past the encumbering bodies of the guards he had knocked out. He saw his immediate opponent duck, saw the hard grin of the killer part his lips as he deliberately lifted his revolver to shoot Wentworth down.

There were the sounds of scuffling inside and strained shouts. Desperately, Wentworth hurled himself forward and saw a hand reaching out of the bus; a hand with a heavy wrench. It swept downward and the gunman's head jarred violently forward. He was falling even as Wentworth's shoulder drove into his belly and Wentworth spilled to the ground with an unconscious man.

"Nice work," he called softly, but he could not pause to make sure that the man inside had been taken care of. He would have to trust his helpers for that. He thought that he could! He pushed to his feet, darted back toward the front of the bus. The rest of the guards at the sanitarium were staring toward him.

He hurled his right gun at the man's face as he fought to get past the prostrated guards.

Even as he strode into sight, some of them were starting down the verandah steps. Their shouts came to his ears.

"Hey, what's the trouble?"

"Some of the mugs came to." Wentworth yelled back. "It's all right. We put them to sleep again!" He made his tones mocking, hard with jeering laughter, and heard the echoes of it come back from the group on the verandah. They turned back casually and Wentworth could face again toward the door of the bus.

The policeman stuck his head out. "Everything's under control, Spider," he said hoarsely. "Now what do we do?"

"Take your time," Wentworth told him in a cool whisper. "Get all the guards together and make sure they stay unconscious for a while. Six of you put on their hats and coats, take their guns. Keep out of sight!"

Presently, Wentworth strolled back toward the door of the bus. "Here's the rest of the plan," he told them quietly. "The mob up there will expect the prisoners to be marched to the sanitarium. We'll do just that. Carry the gunmen with us, two of you to each man. The six who have on the coats and hats of the guards and their guns will walk outside the squad of prisoners. The prisoners must stagger and pretend the gas is still working on them. In other words, the gang up there will see just what they expect. Six men and a bus driver guarding a mob of prisoners who are carrying the ones that got knocked out. When we're close enough I'll give the word... and we'll all attack together! Understand?"

The cop let a slow smile move his thick lips. "Spider," he said.

"I've heard a lot of things about you, and one of them anyway was true. You're a smart guy! We'll take those mugs easy."

IT WAS a bedraggled-looking crew that staggered across the sun-warmed grass a while later. They bunched close together under the guns of seven men and they carried unconscious men swung between them. The guards on the verandah stared toward them and went on with their smoking. It wasn't their job.

There was no hurry in the crossing of the lawn and Wentworth, watching narrowly, thought it must appear entirely convincing. There were plenty of the prisoners who were frightened and it showed in their movements, and there were others whose courage was equal to the encounter and who walked with heads up and shoulders back. That was all as it should be. The crucial moment would come when they were within easy recognition distance, when the men could see that the guards were not their friends. Wentworth quickened his pace until he was beside the policeman, and explained that.

"I want to create a diversion," he said quietly. "It will be dangerous to you. You might even be killed. I want you to make a break for it when I give the word. Keep the mob of prisoners between yourself and the guards on the porch. Start a fight. Start yelling, 'They can't do this to us! We got more men than they have! Come on, men—fight.' That sort of thing. If I figure them right, they'll rush forward and we'll be within reach before they recognize us."

The cop pulled in a slow breath. "I said you was smart, Spider. I'm taking orders."

Wentworth smiled his appreciation. They were now nearing

the guards. He dropped back and waited until only a scant fifty feet separated them from the porch, then he called softly to the cop. Instantly, the officer stopped, turned to the men around him and began to shout.

Wentworth added his voice to the others.

"Hey," he yelled at the guards on the porch. "Rally round, you fools. Give a guy a hand." He ran toward the prisoners, but his eyes were keenly on the guards. They whipped out their guns and charged down to the milling group on the lawn.

Wentworth raced around the front of his contingent, a gun in each fist. When the on-running guards were a bare ten feet from the prisoners, one of them glanced toward Wentworth. His mouth opened in a surprised shout; he whipped his gun around.

"Give it to them, men!" Wentworth shouted, and opened fire.

Eight revolvers were blazing at a dozen men before the words were out of his mouth. For a moment of blank amazement, the gun guards checked their race forward. The surprise was complete and the hammer of the guns of what seemed their own allies robbed them of their judgment. Some of the guards turned to run. Others swung their revolvers to meet the withering hail of bullets—and the policeman led a head-long charge.

It was over almost before it was begun The cop took a bullet through the left arm. He was Wentworth's only casualty. Of the dozen guards who had charged, five were dead and four others badly wounded. The other three were beaten down by the charge of the prisoners.

BUT THERE was no time to exult in the victory. Swiftly, Wentworth assembled his small force, distributed the extra arms and charged into the sanitarium. There were brief flurries of fighting, and one more man was killed by the Spider's swift gun, then it was over.

Savagely, Wentworth ranged through the wards where men and women were convalescing from crippling operations. If he could only find the Wreck! But the man was not here; no one was here save the intimidated cripples and the guards and the fresh prisoners from the buses. There were three surgeons and Wentworth identified them all as missing men from the police lists.

They stood, ashamed and pale, in the surgery where Wentworth confronted them.

"I know why you men have done these things," he said quietly. "Now you will have a chance to undo them. I think we have your skill to thank for the fact that almost all those who have been crippled can be made whole and strong again." He paused, gazing at them steadily. "Of course, the Wreck is holding your families as hostage under threat of torture if you falter in your work. I'm going to ask you just two questions. Is the Wreck coming here—that's the first."

One of the doctors had iron-gray hair and his eyes were worn and suffering, "We don't know," he said quietly. "He never says when he is coming. Usually, when we have a new batch of prisoners he does come to... to say what is to be done to them."

Wentworth nodded, "The other question is this: Who owns this sanitarium?"

The gray doctor frowned. "Apparently, the Wreck owns it

now," he said slowly. "It used to be the property of Doctor Otto Bourse."

"*Bourse!*" Wentworth cried. "Good God, man...."

"I don't mean he has anything to do with it now," the doctor said hurriedly. "I merely answered your question."

Wentworth scarcely heard him. His mind was racing back over the events of recent weeks, trying to see if the great surgeon whom Ernest Hathaway had chosen to head the cripple clinic could be in any way involved. Bourse, he remembered, had been accused of practicing... vivisection....

Rapidly, Wentworth made ready to leave the sanitarium. He put the policeman in charge and ordered him to remain. "If the Wreck comes here," he said quietly, "you will know what to do all right." The cop nodded grimly. "Look, Spider," he said, "no matter what comes of this I'm going to catch hell for not trying to arrest you. I know it wouldn't do me no good to try, but headquarters don't think like that. Meantime, I'm A.W.O.L."

Wentworth nodded. "I'll send a letter to the commissioner," he agreed, "and tell them I took advantage of you when you were unconscious." He grinned abruptly, stuck out his hand. "You're all right, officer. And I think your apprehensions are groundless. If you don't get promoted, I know nothing of Kirkpatrick's mental processes."

The cop's face clouded. "Old Kirk is out of it sir," he said. "That louse, Wentworth...."

WENTWORTH'S GRIN twisted, and he swung away without another word. He had adequate armament and he picked the most powerful of the criminal cars parked at the sanitarium. The cop would see that everyone, including the kidnapped men and women, stayed at the sanitarium for the present. It might help trap the Wreck. It might....

Wentworth's eyes were cold and bitter as he tooled the car out of the parking ranks and started back for New York. He scarcely heard the parting cheers of the people he had saved. It meant nothing, unless he could catch the Wreck, nothing except that the Wreck would, at the first opportunity, snare another crowd of victims. Which was why the Spider would shortly interview Dr. Otto Bourse!

Wentworth knew that the bus driver's garb would make him instantly suspect in New York City so at the first sizable upstate town through which he passed he stopped long enough to purchase a suit of second-hand clothing. Not until he was speeding on again did he realize the weariness that weighted his every movement.

He had hoped against hope that once the sanitarium was located, the whole case would be smashed wide open, and that had failed. There had been a secret hope in his heart, too, that he would find Nita and his brave comrades there—and that had failed. He was utterly alone, a hunted man whether he moved as Richard Wentworth or the Spider. It was characteristic of Wentworth that the thought of deserting the battle, even under such terrific odds, never occurred to him; though he knew that almost certain capture awaited him in the city toward which he sped, and Death itself was entering the gamble with loaded dice....

It was late afternoon when, wearing cheap but neat clothing, Wentworth tooled the confiscated car into the streets of

New York City. He glimpsed the black headlines of newspapers shouting about the wholesale kidnapping, but he did not stop to buy one. His whole attention was centered on reaching the hospital and Dr. Bourse.

The man would be hard to see in the police-guarded special hospital that Ernest Hathaway had set up with Wentworth's contribution. It occupied the score of empty floors in the upper part of the Empire State Building, and it would be hard to conceive of a more difficult place to enter unobserved. He could get into the clinic by pretending to be a cripple, though the fake would soon be discovered when his turn came for examination. Nevertheless, it was the course on which Wentworth had determined. What he did afterward would depend on circumstances....

He parked two blocks away from the building and, pulling a crutch from the back of the car, began to limp on it toward the Empire State. He got no farther than the outer doors, where a cordon of blue-coated police was turning back everyone. Inside the lobby, there also swirled an excited crowd. Wentworth jostled his way into the close-pressed ranks. He felt his blood quickening. Some big thing must have happened to cause such police activity.

"Say, buddy," he put a whine in his voice as he addressed one of the police. "Can't a fellow get up to the hospital? I come all the way from Brooklyn to get to the clinic, and...."

"Nobody's going in," the officer grunted.

"Why not? It's oppression, that's what it is! I got some rights!"

"Pipe down," the cop growled and glared at him. "If I was

144

crippled, I wouldn't like getting inside. They just saw the Wreck in the hospital. And maybe he got out and maybe he didn't!"

Wentworth whispered, "Geez, the Wreck! Me, I'm getting away from here!"

All weariness was gone now. He slung himself through the thick press of the crowd. God alone knew what business the Wreck could have in the hospital itself, but they were mad to think they had trapped him inside. Before such a cordon could have been thrown about the building, the Wreck would have escaped easily. It was the first chance he had had to eliminate any suspect from his list. If Bourse were inside the hospital now....

He snatched a newspaper from a stand and hurried on to his car, thrust the crutch into it. A quick glance showed him that he had been right in assuming that Milhauser would act as police commissioner. Wentworth's face sobered. Kirkpatrick's condition was "critical, unchanged." His eyes went blind with staring, so that he saw not the paper in his hands, but the scene in Kirkpatrick's office when he had left. It was damnable that it should have been friendship for himself that had done this to Kirkpatrick. Obviously, some one had entered to find Kirkpatrick unconscious and had shot him: a cold-blooded deed. Wentworth tried to call back to his memory the image of the outer office when he had strode through it. His eyes narrowed as he recalled that someone had been waiting there, a man... No good. He couldn't recall any aspect of the man he half-remembered.

Wentworth doubled the newspaper in a taut fist and strode to the nearest cigar store where he put in a call for the hospital. He made his voice rasping and peremptory.

145

"Commissioner Milhauser's office calling," he said. "Put on Doctor Bourse."

"Doctor Bourse is not in the hospital, sir," the operator reported.

"Then Mr. Hathaway."

"I'm sorry, sir. He is out, too. I can give you Mr. Temple, but...."

Wentworth slammed up the receiver and strode out of the cigar store and there was a new tension in his stride, a drawing in of thigh muscles and in his shoulders. Bourse and Hathaway were not in the hospital. It might mean nothing at all, but at least neither had an alibi for the Wreck's appearance. He wondered briefly why the Wreck had shown himself in the hospital, then thrust the matter aside. The hospital was closed to him, and hence his plans for confronting Bourse. But there was another trail he could follow, one that should lead him straight to the Wreck himself! He could follow a junk wagon....

THERE HAD scarcely been time before to think of the things he had guessed while invading the cripple lodging-house, but the coincidence of the junk wagon's appearance there and the arrival of orders from the Wreck was too pat to be mere accident. And junk had been loaded into the wagon... Wentworth smiled thinly. Before this, it had been a matter of conjecture as to how the Wreck collected the loot his thousand slaves took for him. Who would think of looking for jewels and stolen money in a junk wagon?

Who... except the Spider!

It took time to reach the lodging-houses and darkness was

gathering in the skies before he saw a junk wagon draw to a halt before one of them and begin to load on what seemed odds and ends from the city's trash cans. When later it moved on, Wentworth followed the clank of its swinging bells through the blackening night. Ultimately, it wandered to the West Side and labored in through the gate of a gaping wooden fence behind which were heaped the hulks of cars, scrap iron; all the salvage of civilization's refuse. Wentworth waited a long while and no one came out. He took his crutch from the back of the car and began to limp his way through the deserted streets. It was a district of coal and lumber yards, of gaunt, windowless warehouses, and the streets were empty of life.

Wentworth swung into the black niche of a wagon doorway and stared toward the junk dealer's shack. Backed against it were the elevators of a coal yard and there, too, a watchman's kiosk held a light. Those two gleaming points were the only evidences of life in all the blackness. On the river a tug hooted mournfully.

Wentworth swore under his breath. Time was skipping past and presently the Spider must call on Dr. Bourse. He might remain in wait here throughout the night and nothing happen; or the junk dealer might start out the next moment on his journey to turn over the loot Wentworth was sure he carried to the Wreck himself. It would be simple enough to invade the shack, but he had no confidence in being able to force a minion of the Wreck to talk. The monster held his slaves in too close a grip. And he would betray his own knowledge of the junk system.

Wentworth swung out of the doorway and started on a slow circuit of the block. It was just possible there was an exit on the other street that he had missed; and that the light was intended as a decoy while the junk dealer slipped away. He turned the corner and was halfway toward the intersecting street when, in the darkness of an alley's mouth, he caught a glimmer that might be a human face. It was instantly gone and Wentworth did not betray by so much as a jerk of his head that he had seen anything.

The place was directly on his path. He swung on toward it, limping more heavily on his crutch. His eyes stabbed into the blackness of the shadows. Was this some sentry of the Wreck? If it were, Wentworth must make sure he did not return to report a prowler!

His crutch tapped out its irregular pace upon the pavement and Wentworth was conscious of the pressure of the twin guns thrust into his waistband. He loosened his coat. More clearly now, he could see into the shadows. There was a hunched figure, crouched there against the wall. A pair of crutches was laid on the earth and... Lord, it was a woman, an old woman with a shawl over her head. Unconsciously, he checked as he stared toward her. She had a beggar's cup in her hand and her legs were pitifully twisted beneath a torn and thread-bare skirt. But what was a beggar doing here? It was still possible that she was a sentry for the Wreck.

Just over her, Wentworth paused, his crutch braced out to steady him, a hand resting casually on the butt of a revolver. She might be a decoy... His eyes slanted into the darkness behind her and found nothing.

"Hell of a lay," he rasped at the woman.

Who do you think's going to give you money here?"

The women mumbled and drew the shawl more closely about her face and Wentworth's eyes sharpened. Why did she want to hide her face?

"Come on," he said roughly, "let's go where there are some bright lights. The crowd will be getting on Broadway soon. A woman and a man together always gets the dough. What do you say?"

"No!" The monosyllable was muffled, and the woman lifted a hand to the shawl at her throat, drew it tight.

Wentworth went taut to the last nerve in his body, and a suffocation gripped him by the throat. That hand… that narrow, graceful hand, and the voice of this old beggar woman! He gripped the crossbar of his crutch until his forearm ached. For moments he could not speak. Slowly, his eyes went once more over the huddled, half-seen body in the shadows, the stooped shoulders, the twisted legs. On the woman's forehead, a wisp of hair caught a gleam from a distant light.

He tried to speak, and his voice caught in his throat. He moved a hesitant hand toward that bowed head, yet did not touch it. He could see the woman's other hand now and it held a small, black automatic under the fringe of her shawl. He dropped the crutch and went down on his knees in the dirt of the alley.

He whispered, "Oh, my God. Nita… Nita, beloved."

He saw the jerk of the woman's stiffening body, but her face swung away, the gun was suddenly presented at his breast.

"Scram," her voice came harshly. Don't try nothing or I'll blow you open. Did you hear me?"

Wentworth laughed, and there was a strangling lump in his

throat. He stretched out his hand and touched hers. Suddenly, fiercely he caught her into his arms. "Oh, my dear, did you think you could fool me? Me?" Roughly, he brushed the shawl from her head, looked down into the sweet face, the deep eyes he knew so well. His heart squeezed in his breast, for the shadows beneath those eyes were real and the lines of pain about her mouth could not be hidden. And he remembered her twisted legs.

"Oh, Dick," Nita whispered. "Why, why did you have to find me?"

Her twisted legs... Wentworth rasped out a violent oath and rage strangled him. He had found her, but too late... too late! The Wreck had done this to her, to Nita! Nita... a *cripple!*

CHAPTER 11
TO SAVE THE CITY

I T WAS a moment of great joy, and of unutterable sadness for Wentworth. It was only presently that he could sufficiently master his white-hot rage against the Wreck and speak, but even then the tremors that ran along his nerves made his voice uncertain and harsh. He knew now why he had never heard from Nita. A cripple, she was unwilling to return to the shelter of his love. But his grief was madness. Proper surgery would mend her twisted legs. Almost always, it was possible. *Almost...* Wentworth thrust the doubt from him savagely. His arms strained Nita against his breast, until she stirred.

"This was madness, Nita," he said brusquely then. "You can be cured. It wasn't brave of you to hide from me. It was foolishness."

Nita laughed uncertainly, "And a bit of vanity, Dick. Just a bit. But listen, dear, there is a new attack planned tonight. At the World's Fair. I tried to warn the police, but I don't think they'll pay any attention to me. I phoned them twice before and they wouldn't believe me."

Wentworth swore softly, his brain racing with the things she had revealed even while his eyes hungrily devoured her. "If only Kirkpatrick were back in the saddle, but it's that fool, Milhauser. I'll have to do something. When is the attack?"

"At midnight, Dick. It's robbery, I think. The Wreck has promised freedom and wealth to any cripple who is injured doing his work for him. That was the message given out at the dormitory earlier tonight. I slipped away... And Dick, Dick, the loot comes in by way of this junk yard."

Wentworth nodded. "Have you ever seen anything carried out of the junk yard?" he asked.

Nita shook her head, her eyes never leaving Wentworth's face. It was as if she could never see enough of it, as if she never expected to see it again. He crouched beside her, an arm about her shoulders and his eyes peered off into the night blindly. His duty lay plainly before him, but he could not leave Nita here— nor could he offer her sanctuary. He was homeless, hunted. He rose abruptly to his feet.

"Come, Nita," he said shortly. "I have a car near here. There's only one thing to do. I've got to reach Kirkpatrick. If he's as ill as they say he is...."

Nita said quietly, "I'm not going, Dick. Sooner or later, they're bound to move the loot from that junk yard, or the Wreck will come there. When he does—" Nita's hand was on the gun that lay in her lap—*"I want to be here!"*

"Nonsense," Wentworth said roughly. "Do you think I'm going to lose you, now that I've found you again?"

Nita smiled up at him, her face a pale blur in the darkness. "No, Dick, you won't lose me. But if you have a duty, I have one, too. You can come back here after you've seen Kirkpatrick. I'll be waiting. I promise."

Wentworth's hands knotted into slow hard fists. If Nita promised to remain, she would, but to leave her here to face a probable battle with the Wreck… Wentworth shook his head. Actually, she would be safer here than with him. The Wreck would not visit the yard when titanic plans were coming to fruition. A wholesale raid on the World's Fair with cripples who would be seeking immolation in order to be free… Wentworth shuddered at the thought. It meant massacre, and behind the screen of the cripples' attack, the Wreck would loot the treasury. He bent toward Nita again.

"Since you promise, my sweet," he whispered. "But don't concentrate too much on the thought that the loot is all stored in the junkyard. It would be madness to leave it there. If nothing is ever carried out of the junk yard, then it must leave in some other way. The coal elevators…" He stiffened with the thought. "By the heavens, I'll bet that's it! The loot comes into the junk yard, is carried off by the coal trucks operating next door."

He felt suddenly at ease about Nita. The Wreck certainly

would not come here and, barring that, she would be safe in her covert.

Nita's hands clung to his through a painful moment, then she released him. "Be careful, Dick, for my sake," she whispered.

"For both our sakes," he assured her, and swung off into the night on his one crutch. There was agony in his heart at the thought of leaving her, even though it increased her safety. He had seen her so briefly after so many long days of struggle and search. He fought with an impulse to insist on her accompanying him. He could not feel at ease about leaving her there. Danger was in the air... He shook his head. It was his emotions working on him, no more. Nita was safe... was safe.

HOWEVER, NITA was never out of his mind as he sent the car racing back across the city. And he still knew that sense of over-weening danger... The hospital in which Kirkpatrick lay was a private institution occupying a half-dozen upper stories in a building near police headquarters. There would be guards, of course, since Kirkpatrick's injury was the result of a murderous attack, but Wentworth already had formed a plan.

He drove his car to the garage hideout where usually he kept the battered coupé which he had been forced to sacrifice in the battle with the Wreck. He found there, in his secret cache, a long length of the silken rope which the police knew as the Spider's web—a line no thicker than a pencil which tested at more than seven hundred pounds.

Thoughtfully, he exchanged the captured revolvers he carried for two of his familiar heavy automatics, and put into the sedan a small make-up tray and the cape and hat of the Spider. He

would return for Nita, but afterward he must throw his strength
into the battle at the Fair Grounds. Hunted though he was, the
presence of the Spider would stiffen the morale of the police,
and throw fear into the raiders of the Wreck!

A block from the hospital, Wentworth abandoned his car and,
with the silken rope wound about his waist, made his way up
the fire-escape of a loft building. A telephone call had already
ascertained Kirkpatrick's room number. He was familiar enough
with the hospital to locate it, and he hurried across irregular
roofs toward the uplifted tower of the hospital building. There
were awnings on the windows and, for the Spider, the rest was
easy. The loop of a rapidly rigged lariat dropped over the hook to
which the awning rope was secured and, with the "web" looped
about his hands, he walked up the side of the building.

Carefully....

A half-dozen minutes later, panting from his exertion, he
clung to the sill of a bathroom window three stories above the
roof he had crossed. The window of what he calculated was
Kirkpatrick's room was a half-dozen feet away. Once more the
lariat looped upward and, with that knotted beneath his arms
for a safety rope, he made the span to the windowsill. A glance
inside assured him that he had come to the right place, but his
heart stabbed him at the sight of Kirkpatrick, white faced and
immobile on the bed. There was uncertainty in the jerky lift and
fall of his breathing, but the nurse, in a chair beside a dim night-
light, was nodding in sleep.

The window was open and Wentworth ducked soundlessly
to the floor, reached the nurse in a long stride. Stiffened fingers

154

prodded the side of her throat. Her head jerked upward, her eyes flicking wide, then she slumped sideways from the chair, unconscious. Wentworth eased her to the floor and bent over Kirkpatrick's bed, staring with grief-pinched features in the face of his friend.

"Kirk," he whispered. "Kirk, it's Dick."

There was no change in the heavy, slow respiration, no twitch of the sleeping face to indicate he had heard. Wentworth tried twice more without response and then he straightened, eyes narrowing. Kirkpatrick was drugged. With a quick stride, he reached the foot of the bed and caught up the chart that hung there. A soundless shout rose to his lips. This was no chart of a man critically wounded… and the name in the space for the attending physician was… *Otto Bourse!*

Cautiously, Wentworth lifted the bedding. Kirkpatrick had been wounded all right, but the bullet-hole apparently was high up in the shoulder and in no way dangerous. Still, it would be impossible to arouse Kirkpatrick from that drugged slumber sufficiently to understand what he had to say. A thin smile touched the Spider's lips. The Wreck planned well, but there was a thing on which he had not planned!

QUIETLY, WENTWORTH locked the door of the room, then caught up the telephone instrument beside the bed. When he spoke, it was with the clipped accents of the man who lay upon the bed. He made his voice weak, blurred as if with illness. That would take care of any deficiency in his imitative ability.

"Police headquarters," he muttered into the phone. "Get

Milhauser to the phone. At once. And don't call any of these confounded asses you call internes. I'm all right."

The call went through swiftly and, moments later, Milhauser was speaking.

"Kirkpatrick calling," Wentworth said faintly. "Of course from the hospital. I've just had a message from a source I trust. The Wreck is raiding the Fair Grounds. Throw all reserves into the area. At once. It's an order; Milhauser. If you doubt the authenticity of it, call back the hospital for confirmation. That's all. I'll be back on the job tomorrow. Ridiculous! My wound is only a scratch!"

He hung up long enough to disconnect, then signaled the operator again. "Get me Doctor Bourse at the Hathaway Emergency Hospital," he said shortly, "and tell him I need him at once. You may relay calls to me during the next half hour. No, I won't see any confounded internes. The nurse is here and she's enough. I've ordered the door locked."

Wentworth left the phone and looked over the articles on the bed-side table, seeking to learn what drug had been given to Kirkpatrick. There was no trace of one. He touched a hand to Kirkpatrick's throat. The pulse was strong, though a little slow. Wentworth's mind was racing wildly.

If he could get Bourse here, he should soon force the truth out of the man. Milhauser would undoubtedly make a display of rushing the reserves to the Fair Grounds and perhaps scare off the Wreck's attack. Wentworth smiled slowly to himself. If matters went well, he would soon have the Wreck in his power. After that… The smile became thin and cold.

It was five minutes later that the phone rang softly and Wentworth delayed in lifting the instrument. "Yes," he said. "Ah, Doctor Bourse is not at the hospital? Then leave a call for him. Did headquarters phone back? Good. Yes, who is it calling now? Miss van Sloan? Yes, yes, put it through quickly."

Fear pounded at him with sledge-hammer blows. His hand trembled on the phone until Nita's voice was whispering swiftly in his ear.

"You were right about the coal yard, Dick," she said. "A truck loaded mostly with loot is starting out now for this address near the Harlem River." She gave him the number and street. "Listen, carefully now, Dick. I crept close to the junk shack and overheard a phone call come in. Afterward; I knocked out the yard man and I'm calling from there now. The attack on the Fair Grounds is a fake. Most of the Wreck's forces are going to be concentrated in Manhattan. A dozen robberies are planned. I have a list of some of them, and…" Her voice leaped to wild speed. "Someone is coming in. It's the Wreck! Good-by, Dick. *Oh, goodbye….*"

Wentworth heard the muted slam of a gun, then a woman's gasped cry. He was already rapidly working the signal bar of the phone. "Police headquarters!" he snapped. "Don't lose a second!"

He had been mad, mad to leave Nita there when he knew that danger threatened her. His mind whirled with fears for her, with the facts that she had thrown at him. Truly, the Wreck planned well!

"Radio room," he snapped. "Kirkpatrick calling." It was hard to imitate the weak, clipped tones of Kirkpatrick when every second of delay might mean the difference between life and death for Nita. Or was it already too late? That gunshot, and the gasp....

"Radio room. Commissioner Kirkpatrick calling. Rush every available radio car to junk yard." He flung out its location. "The Wreck is there. Swiftly, I'll wait."

HE HEARD the pounding energy of the radio announcer's voice as he sent radio cars racing to the scene. Wentworth beat his thigh softly with a knotted fist. They could travel so much more swiftly than he. It would take twenty, twenty five minutes for him to reach his car and speed across the city, but, God, to have to depend on others when Nita was in peril!

There was a part of his mind that was wild with fear, and there was another that pounded on relentlessly with the other information Nita had given him. A fake attack on the Fair Grounds while the Wreck cleaned up in Manhattan. He would delay the second raid until reserves had been drawn to the distant Flushing Meadows where the Fair was situated. He would wait—unless he already knew that they were speeding to the scene. He himself had done that, usurping Kirkpatrick's identity. The blame would be placed solidly on Kirkpatrick's shoulders....

Something like a groan squeezed out between Wentworth's lips.

"Are you all right, sir?" the radio man came back on the wire. "I sent four cars and a detective cruiser. Also a squad car from the nearest precinct."

"Good," Wentworth said. "If they reach there in time, they

will also find Nita van Sloan. She is to be given ample police guard and kept in a safe place. Switch me to Milhauser."

"He's left, sir. I can try to raise him by radio. I think he has your car with the two-way transmitter."

"Right," Wentworth snapped. "This is the message…."

A crash at the door behind him whipped him about in time to see the door driven in by a policeman in uniform. A gun was in his fist, leveled at Wentworth!

Kirkpatrick's crisp voice came from Wentworth's lips. "Drop that gun, you fool!" He turned his back on the policeman and bent over Kirkpatrick. "Here's the phone, Kirk. Go ahead."

In the weak, but clear voice he had used to imitate Kirkpatrick, Wentworth himself spoke into the phone. "Here's the message, operator. The attack on the Fair Grounds will be a fake. The real object of the Wreck is to raid banks and money centers in Manhattan. Milhauser is to make a feint himself at the Fair Grounds. Pick up men on the street, anybody, and send a great fleet of automobiles to the Fair Grounds. The reserves are to be sent quietly into the financial area. Radio cars will converge there and hide in the district to await orders. You will carry on without further instructions from me. Goodnight."

Wentworth straightened and a gun gouged into his spine. "Say, the commissioner wasn't talking!" he said violently. "That was a fake. Say; who are you? The nurse is knocked out!"

Wentworth turned quietly to face the man. He had long ago stripped off disguise and the cop reeled back a stride, the gun leaping up heart-high.

"Wentworth," the man stammered. "Wentworth, and you come back to finish your job. Why, damn you...."

Wentworth saw that his face was tightening with rage, and he knew that within a split-second, the man would fire. He nodded quietly. "Ram Singh, if he moves a finger, drive a knife through his spine," he said.

The cop flinched, started to turn his head and didn't. It made no difference Wentworth's left hand slapped the gun aside and his right crossed to the profiled jaw. The man slumped to the floor and Wentworth passed him in a long bound, reached the doorway. Nurses were running along the hall and he glimpsed a man in a white surgeon's jacket. Wentworth stepped out to confront them.

"Silence," he called quietly. "There's a critically ill man in here. What does all this disturbance mean?"

The interne checked his run, came on at a rapid stride. The nurses fluttered toward the door. Wentworth whipped out an automatic. "You will all be quiet," he said shortly. "Ever so quiet! Doctor, you will revive Mr. Kirkpatrick. He has been drugged. Inside, here. All of you."

They filed past him gingerly, stared down at the unconscious policeman and nurse. The interne bent over the bed. "Why, he hasn't been harmed!" he said uncertainly.

It was the last thing Wentworth heard. He clapped the door shut. "You will stay in there until Mr. Kirkpatrick has revived, and then tell him what has happened," he called softly. "The first person who comes out will be shot!"

HE SPRINTED on soft feet down the hallway to the stairs,

whirled down them. He found the telephone operator's cubicle and, gesturing her brusquely aside, wrecked the board in a half dozen swift movements. He had to prevent further communication with the police until Kirkpatrick had revived sufficiently to take command. Meantime, the Wreck might strike at any moment!

Wentworth's face was a tortured mask as he shot downward in the elevator he summoned to the hospital floor. Nita in the hands of the Wreck again! He dared not hope otherwise, and it was the best that *could* happen. That shot… Wentworth winced with a pain that was actually physical.

Still, he could accomplish no more than the storm of police that had swirled into the neighborhood at his call. If they were in time, Nita was amply protected. If they were too late, his presence could add no single atom to her safety. But it was hard, hard to go into battle from which there was every chance he would not emerge alive and not know… perhaps never know Nita's fate.

There was no hesitancy in Wentworth's movement. He hurled himself into the car, wrenched it from the curb and raced it southward through the city streets, toward the trap that the Wreck had set and might spring at any moment. This was his best chance of meeting the Wreck face to face. If this failed, there was the address to which Nita had reported the coal truck would go. Wentworth's eyes narrowed with enforced thought as he sped through the dark and deserted streets. The police would not yet have heard from the hospital. There was no reason why anyone there should call headquarters until an inquiry had been made.

Wentworth slewed the car to the curb and flung into a drug-store, wedged into a phone booth and put through another call for headquarters. Once more, it was the weak, clipped voice of Kirkpatrick that spoke.

"Send men to throw a tight cordon around the Hathaway Hospital," he ordered, "They are to hold that cordon all night, and arrest anyone who attempts to get into the building. Is that clear? Anyone. That includes Hathaway or Bourse or any other official. That is all, except… switch me to the radio room."

But the radio room had no report yet from the men who had rushed to rescue Nita; Milhauser had taken a car without a two-way transmitter and had not yet phoned headquarters as requested via radio.

Wentworth clashed up the telephone, burst for his car at a dead-run. Radio cars already had been ordered into the financial district, but the seriously needed reserves must wait for Milhauser to countermand his order. Short of that, it was up to the Spider. Wentworth hurled the car on southward and, as he raced, he drew the cape of the Spider about his shoulder and dragged the black, lank wig, the slouch hat down over his brows. There might be time for more disguise, for him to assume the full panoply of the Spider, but he could not wait longer now.

He swerved into Broadway, bore the accelerator to the floor as he flashed past City Hall Square. A few more blocks now, and he would be in the heart of the area the Wreck would attack. A few more blocks… Through the night air, a high thin whistle pierced, and it was echoed by a thousand shouting voices. Suddenly, Wentworth saw the cripples. Scores and hundreds of them poured out into the street from every conceivable hiding place. They popped from behind gravestones in the Trinity churchyard. They leaped from subway entrances, and from shadowed doorways. Wentworth saw a manhole cover lift and a stream of men pour out.

In a brace of seconds, it had become impossible to move without running down one of the crippled men. Wentworth tried to fight the car forward, and he could not. He was stalled. Even as the car dragged to a halt, guns began to speak. The windshield burst in an instant, lead beat a tattoo of death upon the metal sides of the car, The Spider was fighting for his life, and fighting against men whom he could not shoot. They were the victims of the Wreck, as much as his allies.

But the Spider did not hesitate. He flung from the car and began to lash out with his tightly held guns. He fought through the thick press toward the spot where he could see the cars of the Wreck's raiders, the men who would actually commit the robberies. All about him, guns slammed, but more often than not, the bullets struck others of the cripples who attempted to reach him with clubbed crutches, with fists, with clawing hands.

The Spider fought… He tilted back his head and the flat, mocking laughter, the menacing laughter of the Spider poured forth. For in the entrance of the nearest bank, he saw… *the Wreck!*

CHAPTER 12
CAVE OF TORTURE

WENTWORTH'S GUNS swerved toward the target but even as they turned that way, almost as if they moved independently of his own will, he saw that the Wreck was beyond range. He did not fire. A crutch caught him a glancing blow across the shoulder and he staggered, wrenched his foot free from the clutching hands of another cripple.

"Fools!" he shouted at them. "Why do you fight me? There is the man who injured you. There is the man who holds your lives and your loved ones in pawn! Pull him down—and you all go free! Pull down the Wreck, and you go free."

A dozen feet away, he saw a man staring at him with as much amazement as if he had heard human speech for the first time. Another cripple, crutch drawn back across his shoulder for a deadly blow, checked to hear the Spider's words. He poured them out in his deeply resonant voice, and as he spoke he raced toward the spot where the Wreck stood, calmly directing the movements of his men. Police sirens began their wailing, but the notes died quickly. How could the police race to the scene when the streets were cluttered with humanity? Even if they ran down some, the very bodies of the victims would check the wheels of their cars.

"Pull down the Wreck," Wentworth shouted again. "There is the man who crippled you. There is the man who holds you in slavery. Kill him—and you are free!"

A few hoarse shouts echoed him, then a solid volume of

sound as one cripple and then another caught up the fierce cry. "Kill, kill, kill the Wreck."

Wentworth glanced swiftly about him. White, twisted faces were turning toward that doorway where the Wreck stood calmly. Those faces were riven by pain, but it was another thing that was putting the glitter into their eyes, that made their voices the shrieks of madmen. These men were, almost without exception, under the influence of drugs. In part, it explained how the Wreck ruled them, but it made them unstable and fickle in their allegiance. If Wentworth could turn them into a weapon in his own hand....

He was almost within pistol-shot of the Wreck now and his guns were tense and ready in his hands; his fists ached with clutching. A little way farther, a half-dozen more strides and he could shoot with accuracy. Even now, he might risk a shot... No, no, he must make sure. The Wreck was staring toward him, toward the tossed fists and clubbed crutches of the mob. He turned his head almost contemptuously, and another man stepped forward from the shadows of the doorway.

Screams broke out among the mob of cripples. They wheeled and tried to run. They fought against the pressure that was driving them forward, for that man in the doorway held a machine-gun in his hands, and there was a brassy smile on his mouth. The gun began to hammer....

As casually as a man might water a lawn, the killer sprayed his leaden death upon the mob. Men fell in screaming convulsions, or pitched motionless to the pavement. A wide swath of them patched the street and sidewalk. Madness gripped the mob; the

165

insanity of terror. They tried to climb the walls of buildings, they tried to burrow into the asphalt of the street. Mercilessly, the machine gun swayed back a second time.

With the first sputter of the machine gun, Wentworth flung himself prone to the earth and, instants later, the path was clear before him save for the few who still kicked and struggled against the agony in their vitals. Wentworth tipped the muzzles of his automatics high and began to shoot. The range was nearly a hundred and fifty yards. The guns would carry that far, but it wanted a longer barrel for accuracy than his weapon possessed. Both guns hammered together in his fists and their flames lit up the faces of the dead and dying. He swiveled the muzzles slightly as he fired and saw the machine-gun stagger, jerk to a second hit and pitch face-down on the top step of the bank entrance.

The Wreck darted back out of sight and Wentworth was instantly on his feet and running forward at top speed. His guns were half-emptied, but there was no time to reload. He caught the glint of gun-steel thrust around a column and pitched to earth. There was plenty of cover here, the cover of men already dead. Their bodies formed a bulwark... and a machine-gun began to speak again.

BEHIND HIM, Wentworth could catch again the wailing of sirens, then the heavy slam of police guns. The cops were coming on afoot. He wondered dimly if the police reserves were yet on the way, but there was no answer to that. All sound was blotted out by the hammering of the near-by machine-gun. The body behind which he crouched jerked to the prod of leaden fingers.

The bullets made small thudding sounds or smacked when they glanced off stone to shrill off into space.

Wentworth had time to spare to reload his automatics and he did it, huddled close against the pavement. When the deluge of screaming gun-steel slackened for a moment, he peered toward the bank. The gunner was peeping out to see what havoc he had wrought. He did not see. One of Wentworth's guns jerked against a stiff wrist, and the man's head wrenched back out of sight for an instant before he pitched, kicking, to the earth.

Before any other man could take up the machine-gun, Wentworth was up and sprinting for the doorway. He checked. Out of sight around the column that flanked the entrance, and waited, listening tautly. He heard nothing for long moments and then something metallic clanked on the doorstep and toppled, wobbling like a great black egg, toward the column. A cry lifted in Wentworth's throat and he dived between column and stone wall an instant before the hand grenade let go.

Flying steel screamed through the air and the concussion pinned Wentworth, limp and motionless, against the wall. If the men of the Wreck had struck at that moment, Wentworth would have been finished. They did not strike. None of them showed himself at the gaping doors of the bank with its bomb-fragment shattered glass.

Presently, Wentworth could force his stunned body into action. He staggered toward the interior of the bank, and nothing, no one moved. Light filtered in through a narrow swinging door and Wentworth sprinted toward it, peered out into a street.

There was nothing here either, not even the prostrate bodies of cripples. No auto was in sight; no motor sounded.

Wentworth swore under his breath as he crept cautiously from the bank. No bank-wrecking crew could disappear so quickly without special means. Wentworth's eyes flashed everywhere, seeking nothing specific, seeking only movement. They found it. In the middle of the street, where a patch of darkness lay upon the pavement, there came the glint of metal. Wentworth laughed aloud as he flung his lead. He heard the muffled cry of a man and the dull clangor of falling iron and, moments later, he stood over a disarranged manhole. This, then, was the way they had fled!

Violently, Wentworth wrenched at the manhole cover, and it came up in his hands. He tipped it on edge, rolled it toward the curb—and a gust of hot wind picked him up and hurled him through the air. He was aware of glaring light on the flanking buildings that soared to intolerable brightness and died. He felt the ground reach up and batter him with a thousand flailing clubs and then he lay still while strength drained from him. He knew dully that a bomb had been set off in the manhole well an instant after he had turned aside to get rid of the cover.

He owed his life to that split-second delay. The Wreck was escaping with his plunder, and Wentworth could do nothing about it. He could not even move. He was fully conscious of what went on about him, but there was no power to so much as shift his hand where it rested upon the pavement.

Wentworth realized that the concussion had momentarily killed his motor nerve connections. It would pass as suddenly as it had come, or it would never pass. Wentworth knew an instant of deadly fear. God, had that blast broken his back? His mind reeled away from deliberate thought and suddenly he was remembering Nita's voice over the phone and the sweetness of her face as he had held her there in the dark. Nita… Where was she now? He had failed, but Nita….

Wentworth fought the haziness of his mind, brought all his will to bear on something as unimportant as moving his right hand. He watched his right hand with an aching intensity that excluded every other sound, every other thought. His lips turned in upon themselves with bitter compression. The sweat started on his temples… and the hand moved. That was the beginning, but it was fifteen minutes before, fumblingly, Wentworth could drive his exhausted body to its feet. He staggered like a drunken man and, passing a shop window, he saw that the cape and hat had been stripped from him and his coat hung in shreds about his body….

THE NIGHT was crazy with police sirens now. They were coming all right, coming after the looting was completed and the Wreck had escaped. But they might be in time to catch the Spider. Undoubtedly, they would come in time to catch the Spider. Wentworth found his car and flung himself in behind the wheel. His arms moved with incredible slowness as he got the engine going and sent the sedan roaring westward toward the river. He ground the accelerator into the floor and, sweeping downhill, the sedan gained speed at an incredible rate. Wentworth was not watching the speedometer dial. He didn't have a light burning. But had he seen it, he would have seen the needle hover to ninety and creep on.

The sirens and all other sound died out in the shriek of the wind and the howl of the racing motor. He jiggled the steering-gear in a racing turn that sent him skittering half across the hundred-foot width of West Street. He missed a steel pillar of the elevated roadway by inches. A spot of red flame winked at him from a parked car and, off to his left, there was a sputter of blue-violet that was a submachine gun coughing. But Wentworth was traveling nearly a hundred and fifty feet a second. If they hit the car at all he didn't hear the impact.

A car swerved into the roadway ahead of him, started to block his way, and went crazy. It skittered aside in the split second that Wentworth's unwavering grip on the steering wheel sent him past. He felt the thrust of wind like a blow and heard a crash faintly behind him. He did not look back.

Laughter began to pump at Wentworth's chest. Pursuit? What did he care? He was racing to throw the last dice that were given him to cast. If this failed… He was a little mad with the blasts that had shaken him, with the intoxication of the wind. An inch turn on the steering-gear sent him in a wild sweep up the ramp to the overhead drive. Lights blurred past him. The tires moaned and his breath was driven back into his lungs. There was a hot oil smell from the engine and it was good.

Fumblingly, from the recesses of his mind, he dragged out the address that Nita had given him, the place to which a coal truck was carrying the loot of the Wreck. His thought processes still were fuddled, but he knew that if the police failed, he would find Nita there. Simple, wasn't it? A coal truck starting for the Wreck's lair, and next door a girl who had betrayed the Wreck. It had been madness to hope that the police would reach her in time. Madness.

The car ripped from the highway and began to slice across the upper West Side. Wentworth's speed was moderated now, but the grim set expression of his face was unchanged. A tattered man, his countenance streaked with the black of explosions, his teeth gleaming between drawn-back lips, he drove with rock steady hands. It seemed mechanical that, now and again as he drove, one hand should leave the wheel to rest for a moment on a black gun-butt at his waist.

He whirled a corner and the motor idled. The temperature register of the engine was red to the top of its glass tube and steam was jetting out beneath the radiator cap. Wisps of white swirled back through the broken windshield. Wentworth's eyes combed the street ahead and found what he sought—a coal truck backed to the curb. The body was tipped high and coal was racketing down the chute, through a manhole. Automatically, Wentworth's eyes took in the name on the truck's side. Check. The car swerved to the curb and the brakes were slow in gripping. It slammed against the wheel of the truck and Wentworth reeled to the pavement. He heard an angry shout and the driver came around the tailgate.

He saw Wentworth and paused. He was bent forward at the waist with the suddenness of his stop, his arms flexed at his sides. His eyes stared wide and wide. A small whimpering sound came from his lips and he jerked an arm convulsively.

Wentworth stood facing him and waited while that hand found a gun and started to wrench it out. Then Wentworth drew. His bullet picked the man's feet up off the walk, bent him double and slammed him down hard on the walk. The man's knees drew up against his belly. All his body tightened to the shock of lead and then he was limp, dead.

Wentworth's feet fumbled for the curb and he stared down into the manhole. The coal was still racketing down, but it did not fall with the soft impact of stone. It continued to rattle against metal. A bundle wrapped in canvas shot down the chute and vanished. Wentworth laughed shortly. He jumped into the air and went down through the chute feet first!

HIS FEET hit a wall of smooth metal and his body bent to the thrust. He was through the manhole, but he was still traveling through a metal tube. It bent back under the street. Wentworth's lips were still taut against his teeth. His mind worked in smooth flashes, without conscious effort. It had been obvious that the door would not be dumped into a cellar like that. Too easy, if the coal wagon should be traced, for the police to recover it. The hammer of the coal upon metal told him the rest. He didn't know where he was headed, but of one thing he was sure. Wherever it was, it would bring him to the lair of the Wreck.

The tube ended sharply and he shot out into space, landed in a heap upon a pile of coal. He heard a man's hoarse shout and came up to his knees. He was in a cylindrical cavern, walled with muddy brick and lit by the flaring flames of torches. Two men were staring at him. They turned and began to run. They ran wildly, with their arms flung high, their legs pumping wildly and their shouts raced before them.

Wentworth lifted the automatic... and didn't fire. He pushed to his feet and began to sprint. His legs drove like pistons. He was flying, not running. The men seemed to be standing still. The cylindrical cavern—but it was an old sewer wasn't it?—made a slow turn to the left and Wentworth reached it almost simultaneously with the men.

He reached out his gun and slammed the muzzle across the back of the nearest neck. The man's head went down more quickly than his body. He skidded on his face and his legs twisted awkwardly high before they flopped sideways and began to jerk like the legs of a frog in a hot frying-pan. Wentworth's left hand reached out and gripped hard on the neck of the second man. He got the human shield before him just as the guns began to speak.

Before him, the tunnel widened into a well from which three other circular tunnels pushed out their black arms. There were three men in that chamber, and one woman. The woman dangled from ropes that stretched up into the darkness above, and there were weights on her feet. The woman was Nita!

Bullets were plucking at the man whom Wentworth held before him. He could feel their thrust against the stiffness of his wrist. He paid no attention. There was a fourth figure that faded into the blackness of one of the tunnels and he knew that hunched silhouette, that reptilian thrust of the head. It was the Wreck. But he had no bullets to waste. Wentworth skidded to a halt, the man's body still before him though it dangled with the limpness of death. Three times his automatic dropped into line and three times leaped upward against the rigidity of his wrist.

The first man took the bullet through his open, shouting mouth, and his head jerked backward as if it had no connection with his body. When it struck the wall, the whole body leaned like that, arching backward like a bow. When it fell, there was red on the wall. The second man took the lead through the heart and died in a squirming knot on the floor.

The third man was turning away to run when the bullet caught him. It pinned his left arm to his side and ploughed on. The man reeled sideways three skating, falling steps before he hit the wall. He doubled then, with the painful slowness of a rheumatic, while he tried to cough the blood out of his lungs… and coughed his life along with it.

Wentworth was bounding forward even while the last two bullets sped. The gun kicked once more in his hand and the rope that held the heavy weight to Nita's tortured, twisted legs thudded sullenly to the earth. Nita did not move. Her head sagged backward between her up-straining arms and the soft curling of her hair was a mockery to the rigidity of her tormented body.

For all his haste, Wentworth's arm closed tenderly about her. He slashed through the ropes that held her prisoner and as he lifted her down, Nita's eyes fluttered open for a moment and her tight-drawn lips softened in a smile.

"Dick," she whispered. "I knew you'd come."

Wentworth clutched her savagely to his breast while his wild-straining eyes quested through the tunnel mouths. The

Wreck had been there, but the Wreck had gone. Wentworth laughed harshly.

He knew where the Wreck would go. He must build his alibi now for this horror. He must get back into the Hathaway Emergency Hospital… and the police would be keeping guard over the entrances. Among so many other violent necessities, the acting commissioner would have forgotten to cancel that order at least. The rest did not matter… not now.

WENTWORTH FOUND an iron ladder bolted to the side of the sewer and climbed up it with Nita, unconscious, across his shoulder. He knew no weariness, and his body was a thing of steel and whipcord. It would never tire again. There were people in the street above when he pushed open the cover of the sewer. They took a single look at him and fled, wildly, into the night.

Wentworth moved on steady, automaton legs to his car, laid Nita gently on the seat and a second later was wrenching in a tire-screaming turn to race back downtown again. Yet there was no violent need for hurry now. Better to go slowly. The police guard would hold strong for the little added time he needed. And he did not want some officious traffic officer to stop him. He would not permit it.

While he drove, he sprung the emptied clip from his gun, fumbled another from his pocket and thrust it home in the butt of the automatic. He counted carefully in his mind. Yes, there was a good shell in the chamber.

It was directly in front of the Empire State Building, in the no-parking area that he stopped the car. He clambered to the pavement and, as he lifted Nita, she stirred faintly and opened her eyes again.

"It's all right, dear," Wentworth said. "I'm going to kill the Wreck." He meant to speak gently, but there was a flatness and a fierceness in his voice that fell strangely on the quiet of the street. It was deserted. Across the entrance of the Empire State stood four policemen, but Wentworth walked toward them.

"You have your orders from Kirkpatrick," he said flatly. "They were to arrest every man who tried to get into the building. What officials of the hospital have you taken?"

The cop stared at him and there was a dazed look upon his face, but words came from him as if unconsciously. It was in moments like these that the Spider earned the title that had been his through the years of his battling. He was a Master of Men and no one barred his passage or forbade him what he demanded.

"We got Hathaway and Bourse," the cop said thickly. "Both of them just showed up."

Wentworth smiled thinly and walked through the cordon.

"Hey," the cop called. Wentworth made no reply, but walked steadily into the lobby of the building with Nita in his arms. In the lobby Bourse and Hathaway were arguing with officers who had them in charge. Wentworth glanced at the courageous set of Hathaway's head and the swift welcome of his smile. He gazed into the surgeon's narrow, steady eyes and took in the stoop of his high shoulders. Either of these men, with the proper disguise, could be the Wreck, and they had been caught coming into the hospital.

"Bring them to the conference room of the hospital," Wentworth said shortly. "Kirkpatrick's orders."

"We haven't had them, sir," a sergeant protested.

Wentworth was moving toward the elevators. The sergeant hesitated. "Maybe you'd better go up, gentlemen."

"You're damned right we'll go up," Dr. Bourse snapped, "and you'll answer for this, my man."

Hathaway's voice boomed, "After all, Doctor… we don't know the reasons."

The conference room was resplendent with the trappings that had decorated Hathaway's office at the Jupiter plant. There was a desk and a half-dozen chairs. There was a chart on the wall that showed the progress of the drive for funds and another that showed the number of crippled patients discovered and treated. There was a second door in the room and Wentworth glanced toward it.

"That door leads where?" he asked.

"A closet… Why, good God, it's Wentworth!" Hathaway's strong face flushed. "You damned assassin! You walked right past the police, but I'll… Good God, would you shoot me?"

Wentworth, smiling thinly from behind the loom of his automatic, said, "I can tell you better in a few moments. I think we need your assistant, Temple. Call him."

INDIGNANTLY, HATHAWAY lifted his voice to call Temple and no one answered. Presently, a man thrust his head in through the door to the outer room. "Mr. Temple was here a short while ago, sir," he said. "I don't see him now."

"Find him," Hathaway ordered.

"There are several things I want to know," Wentworth said softly. "Doctor Bourse, a sanitarium you once owned is now the hideout of the Wreck. It is there he has crippled these hundreds of men. What do you know about it?"

Dr. Bourse smiled with a curt movement of his lips that seemed to hurt him. "Nothing at all. I sold the sanitarium through a real estate agency."

"Doctor Bourse." Wentworth's voice was dead calm. "Your name is on Kirkpatrick's chart. He is not seriously wounded as the newspapers say. He was kept under dope."

Bourse shrugged his high shoulders. He was lighting a cigar, casually. "The report of serious injury was his own idea."

Wentworth felt, all at once, the weight of the task, and it was like weariness in his bones. He had no evidence to single one of these men out from the other, nothing to prove that one was the Wreck.

Nita said, quietly, "I can identify the Wreck, Dick."

Wentworth swung toward her and—the lights blacked out in the room. It was as sudden and complete as blindness. Wentworth dove through air toward Nita's chair and carried it over to the floor and a streak of flame split the darkness. Wentworth fired at the flash and the room rocked with the double concussion. A man groaned and the lights came on.

Bourse was gripping his right arm and his face was twisted with pain. Hathaway lay prone upon the floor and there was a narrow panel swinging open in the wall. Behind it hung a black robe and a black hat and on the floor was a thing like a rat cage that Wentworth knew was an artificial hump. Hathaway's hand was almost inside the secret opening in the wall and there was a growing red swelling on his forehead.

Wentworth laughed sharply and with a long bound reached the door of the closet which was just behind Bourse. He yanked open the door and leaped aside in the same instant… but nothing happened. There was a man crumpled on the floor and as Wentworth stared at him, the man lifted his head.

"Thanks," he whispered. "I was almost out. It's close in here."

It was Temple, Hathaway's assistant, and there were handcuffs on his wrists. Wentworth pulled him out and swiftly searched him, peered into the closet. There was no gun on the floor either. Wentworth backed away from him and crouched beside Nita. Hathaway was stirring.

"Hathaway," Wentworth said softly. "You designed this office. You alone would be able to build in a secret closet, but you were caught coming into the place and there must be a secret entrance, too. Perhaps an elevator."

Hathaway said, dizzily, "There is such an elevator, but I never used it. I had no reason to come in secretly. What in hell are you talking about?"

Nita was whispering into Wentworth's ear and a cold smile played across his lips. He said, almost softly, "I'm going to ask you three gentlemen to lift your hands, high above your heads. At once!"

The three men stared at him and slowly began to lift their hands.

"High up," Wentworth whispered. Reach for the ceiling. Shall I tell you why? Miss van Sloan has several times met the

Wreck face to face, gentlemen, and it is a fact that, due no doubt to some past injury, *the Wreck cannot raise his hands above his shoulders.*"

The hands of Hathaway and Bourse shot high above their heads, but Temple… a snarl twisted his mouth and, suddenly, he had freed his hands of the manacles! He was leaping toward Wentworth. Wentworth laughed and, as the man sprang upon him, he stepped aside and struck Temple across the mouth.

"It is simple now that suspicion is turned toward you, Temple," he said. "You actually carried out Hathaway's orders to make the changes in this building, so you installed the secret panel. You tried to frame him a moment ago when you turned out the lights and struck him beside the secret closet. You see, Temple, *Hathaway had no reason to be there.*"

Temple had reeled back toward the broad windows under Wentworth's blow. There was a streak of blood at his mouth corner. He stooped toward the floor and there was suddenly a gun in his hand. Its blast and the explosion of Wentworth's gun were simultaneous.

Temple was a reeling figure with one high flung arm and a distorted face. He was silhouetted against the broad windows and, even now in his dying moment, he could not jerk his left hand higher than his shoulder. Wentworth deliberately fired again.

The bullet struck high in the chest and it snapped Temple backward a full six feet. The window was only a yard behind him… The tinkle and crash of the breaking glass was the only sound after that shot. The warm air of the July night wafted in through the broken window, and the sparkle of the stars was very close and Temple was… gone. Wentworth had his left hand pressed to his hip.

"No, no," he said, "it's nothing, Nita. Just a flesh wound." He laughed sharply, and the sound was bitter and mocking, punctuated by a sudden thud that echoed softly upward from the outer night. "But the Wreck… I think he chose his name well."

POPULAR HERO PULPS AVAILABLE NOW:

THE SPIDER

- ❏ #1: The Spider Strikes — $13.95
- ❏ #2: The Wheel of Death — $13.95
- ❏ #3: Wings of the Black Death — $13.95
- ❏ #4: City of Flaming Shadows — $13.95
- ❏ #5: Empire of Doom! — $13.95
- ❏ #6: Citadel of Hell — $13.95
- ❏ #7: The Serpent of Destruction — $13.95
- ❏ #8: The Mad Horde — $13.95
- ❏ #9: Satan's Death Blast — $13.95
- ❏ #10: The Corpse Cargo — $13.95
- ❏ #11: Prince of the Red Looters — $13.95
- ❏ #12: Reign of the Silver Terror — $13.95
- ❏ #13: Builders of the Dark Empire — $13.95
- ❏ #14: Death's Crimson Juggernaut — $13.95
- ❏ #15: The Red Death Rain — $13.95
- ❏ #16: The City Destroyer — $13.95
- ❏ #17: The Pain Emperor — $13.95
- ❏ #18: The Flame Master — $13.95
- ❏ #19: Slaves of the Crime Master — $13.95
- ❏ #20: Reign of the Death Fiddler — $13.95
- ❏ #21: Hordes of the Red Butcher — $13.95
- ❏ #22: Dragon Lord of the Underworld — $13.95
- ❏ #23: Master of the Death-Madness — $13.95
- ❏ #24: King of the Red Killers — $13.95
- ❏ #25: Overlord of the Damned — $13.95
- ❏ #26: Death Reign of the Vampire King — $13.95
- ❏ #27: Emperor of the Yellow Death — $13.95
- ❏ #28: The Mayor of Hell — $13.95
- ❏ #29: Slaves of the Murder Syndicate — $13.95
- ❏ #30: Green Globes of Death — $13.95
- ❏ #31: The Cholera King — $13.95
- ❏ #32: Slaves of the Dragon — $13.95
- ❏ #33: Legions of Madness — $12.95
- ❏ #34: Laboratory of the Damned — $12.95
- ❏ #35: Satan's Sightless Legion — $12.95
- ❏ #36: The Coming of the Terror — $12.95
- ❏ #37: The Devil's Death-Dwarfs — $12.95
- ❏ #38: City of Dreadful Night — $12.95
- ❏ #39: Reign of the Snake Men — $12.95
- ❏ #40: Dictator of the Damned — $12.95
- ❏ #41: The Mill-Town Massacres — $12.95
- ❏ #42: Satan's Workshop — $12.95
- ❏ #43: Scourge of the Yellow Fangs — $12.95
- ❏ #44: The Devil's Pawnbroker — $12.95
- ❏ #45: Voyage of the Coffin Ship — $12.95
- ❏ #46: The Man Who Ruled in Hell — $13.95
- ❏ #47: Slaves of the Black Monarch — $13.95
- ❏ #48: Machineguns Over the White House — $13.95
- ❏ #49: The City That Dared Not Eat — $13.95
- ❏ #50: Master of the Flaming Horde — $13.95
- ❏ #51: Satan's Switchboard — $13.95
- ❏ #52: Legions of the Accursed Light — $13.95
- ❏ #53: The City of Lost Men — $13.95
- ❏ #54: The Grey Horde Creeps — $13.95
- ❏ #55: City of Whispering Death — $13.95
- ❏ #56: When Thousands Slept in Hell — $13.95
- ❏ #57: Satan's Shakles — $14.95
- ❏ #58: The Emperor From Hell — $14.95
- ❏ #59: The Devil's Candlesticks — $14.95
- ❏ #60: The City That Paid to Die — $14.95
- ❏ #61: The Spider at Bay — $14.95
- ❏ #62: Scourge of the Black Legions — $14.95
- ❏ #63: The Withering Death — $14.95
- ❏ #64: Claws of the Golden Dragon — $14.95
- ❏ #65: The Song of Death — $14.95
- ❏ #66: The Silver Death Reign — $14.95
- ❏ #67: Blight of the Blazing Eye — $14.95
- ❏ #68: King of the Fleshless Legion — $14.95
- ❏ *NEW:* #69: Rule of the Monster Men — $16.95

THE WESTERN RAIDER

- ❏ #1: Guns of the Damned — $13.95
- ❏ #2: The Hawk Rides Back from Death — $13.95
- ❏ #3: Gun-Call for the Lost Legion — $13.95
- ❏ #4: The Law of Silver Trent — $13.95
- ❏ #5: The Gun-Prayer of Silver Trent — $13.95
- ❏ #6: Silver Trent Rides Alone — $13.95

G-8 AND HIS BATTLE ACES

- ❏ #1: The Bat Staffel — $13.95

CAPTAIN SATAN

- ❏ #1: The Mask of the Damned — $13.95
- ❏ #2: Parole for the Dead — $13.95
- ❏ #3: The Dead Man Express — $13.95
- ❏ #4: A Ghost Rides the Dawn — $13.95
- ❏ #5: The Ambassador From Hell — $13.95

DR. YEN SIN

- ❏ #1: Mystery of the Dragon's Shadow — $12.95
- ❏ #2: Mystery of the Golden Skull — $12.95
- ❏ #3: Mystery of the Singing Mummies — $12.95

RED FINGER

- ❏ *NEW:* #1: Second-Hand Death — $24.95

www.ingramcontent.com/pod-product-compliance
Lightning Source LLC
Chambersburg PA
CBHW020331260626
47156CB00004B/1477